I0662446

Believe In Love

Cauldron Falls, Volume 1

Solara Gordon

Published by THE EARTH MOVED, LLC, 2023.

BELIEVE IN LOVE

First edition. March 29, 2023.

Copyright © 2023 Solara Gordon.

ISBN: 979-8986032559

Written by Solara Gordon.

Also by Solara Gordon

Cascade Bay
Love Reborn
Reunited By Choice
Love's Triple Play

Cauldron Falls
Believe In Love

Peyton Corners
Falling for You
Caught by Love's Slow Burn

Standalone
A Heart's Desire
To Love You Again
To Love You Again

Watch for more at https://solaragordon.com/.

Every book starts somewhere. Nick and Sandra's story grew out of a fun interactive improv story item from my newsletter, You Decide What Comes Next. As Nick and Sandra's story progressed, it became clear a new series was forming. Welcome to Cauldron Falls, where full moon matches and Sadie Hawkins dances ignite sparks and join hearts as the magic of love fills the air. The following people helped guide and create Nick and Sandra's journey to Believe in Love:

Cathy Mesaric Bartlett

Karen Wright

Steph K Coutts

Christine Heydt

Chandra Woolson

Rebecca Moninghoff

Kathy Brown

Denise Gaff

Sissy Daniel Johson

Thank you for your input, cheers and continued readership. Here's to the next Cauldron Falls romance!

ONE

"How good a fake are you?" Nick Morgan set his half-empty wine glass on the table and slid into the booth opposite Sandra Cunningham.

"How good am I a what?" Sandra stared at him, her mouth open.

"A fake. You know, pretending to be something you're not." Nick opened the menu in front of him. He glanced over the specials, closed the menu and laid it on the table. Sandra sat quietly, gawking at him, her mouth closed. Garrett's suggested opening line hit pay dirt alright. Paydirt that was two-thirds manure and a third disbelief.

Sandra swiped her sweaty palms on her jeans. *Talk about caught off-guard!* Good thing she'd swallowed her wine before Nick reached the table. Leeana hadn't mentioned anything like this when she said Nick had contacted her asking how to get in touch. Was Nick trying to be funny?

"Why would I want to do that?' Sandra sipped her wine. Had Leeana told him about their recent discussion?

"Well. . .sometimes you need to bluff your way through things...you know." Nick opened the menu again.

"No, I don't know. Bluff I've done when I wasn't completely sure about something. Usually, understanding a new concept or technique, not much more than that." Sandra set her wine glass down on the table. "How good a fake are you?"

Nick slowly exhaled. He wasn't damn good at faking anything with this conversation. He and Sandra weren't strangers. They'd known each other for several years. They'd dated off and on during high school and beyond, been occasional friends with benefits, and accompanied each other to parties and social occasions. Why the hell was it so hard to ask her to go with him to his cousin Paulina and Jackson's wedding?

"I don't know. It's not something I set out to do. There's a first time for everything, I guess." Nick pushed the menu aside.

"Are you bullshitting me? If you don't want to be here, it's okay." Sandra held up her hand. "Garrett and Mary love trying to fix people up. They've tried with you and me before."

"No bs. I need a favor. Garrett suggested a straightforward approach. Except his opening line crashed." Nick pointed to the waiter approaching the table. "Let's order, then I'll explain."

Sandra nodded. Nick pricked her curiosity with his needed a favor line. Talk about coincidence. She needed one too. "Yeah, I'm hungry."

"Good evening. What can I start you with?" The waiter laid his pad on the table. "The taquitos and guacamole dip is going fast tonight. The spring rolls are popular too."

Nick pointed to one of the appetizers on the menu. "I'll start with the spring rolls and spicy corn fritters, please. Bring enough sauce for two. For my entrée, the Mahi Mahi tacos with extra pico de gallo, sour cream and shredded cheese with a side of refried beans and rice."

"And you, ma'am?" The waiter turned to Sandra.

"Bring the half order of his appetizer. We're sharing his and mine. My entrée is the shredded chicken enchiladas minus the jalapenos. Beans and rice side along with extra pico de gallo, sour cream and cheese sauce. I'd like some water with two pieces of lime, please."

Sandra set her empty wine glass close to the edge of the table. "Nick, do you want water?"

"Yeah, I'm done with my wine too." Nick placed his glass next to hers. "I drove tonight. One glass is my limit."

Sandra smiled and nodded. "Mine too. Gotta keep our wits about us."

The waiter confirmed their orders and walked away. Sandra took her cell phone out of her purse and laid it on the table. "You asked

something earlier and I gave you a flip answer. I'd like to ask a question if you don't mind."

Nick leaned back against the booth. He laid his arm on the back of the booth seat cushion. "Sounds like we both got questions. I asked the first one. Your turn."

"Why do you need to fake something?" Sandra glanced at her phone. Her question made as much sense as Nick's had. Faking sounded naughty and sneaky. Pretending was . . .make believe...play-acting. . .fantasizing. Nick showed up in some of her hottest favorite fantasies. Helped her run down her favorite vibrator's batteries. Got her hot and bothered in all the usual places. Sandra slowly inhaled, laid her palms flat on the table, hoping the coolness of the table would detract her conscience from flashing images from last night's dreams.

Nick pressed his lips together. Garrett said Sandra was his best option. The one that would go along with the idea. The one person who knew him the best. The one who could make his family believe what they had was real. How authentic did it need to be? Gram mentioned he and his fiancee staying at her place with no need for separate beds since they were engaged during their stay for Paulina and Jackson's wedding. Knowing Gram, she'd be checking for used condoms and wanting to know how soon her great-grandbabies would arrive. Nick inhaled slowly, pressing each finger of both hands against his leg. Counting wasn't going to make this any easier.

Sandra turned him on in high school and from the moment they'd shared a slow dance three years ago. Her snuggled up in his arms, a hair's breadth away from him. Her shoulder-length strawberry blonde hair. Hazel eyes that changed colors with her mood. Azure as they quenched their passion. Golden green like a cat's eyes when her temper flared. Curves in all the right places. Places where his hands and lips wanted to taste and touch. Thinking thoughts that kept his hard-on from nudging her hadn't been easy. Six months later, the revelation they found each other hot and desirable during a game of truth or dare spin the bottle at a friend's cookout. Three months later, they'd kissed and—-Nick looked up. Friends with possible occasional—no, Sandra wouldn't say okay. . .would she?

"My mom and gram. . ." Nick hesitated, wondering if Sandra would believe they were still nagging him about kids and marriage.

Nick picked up his wine glass and swirled the remaining wine in the glass. The only unmarried son in the current generation of the Morgan family line. His mom and gram fussed and talked about their grandchildren and great-grandchildren. With ten apiece, you would think they had enough. No. He was the oddball. The remaining single grandchild Gram swore she would see married before she went to her reward. The only male non-magic in twenty-five generations. So what if he got the quirky gene that made him stand out at family functions. Big deal. If he brought a date, she'd be non-magic too. He hadn't told Sandra about his family.

"Still?" Sandra asked.

"Yes, still." Nick nodded as he continued. "You'd think they'd wise up after while."

Sandra smiled, shaking her head. "We never grow up for our parents. Mine aren't as big on grandkids. The gotta find someone and settle down part, *oh yeah*."

"One more thing we have in common. Maybe Garrett was right." Nick grinned, leaning forward. "I think I need to reword my earlier question."

"Oh?" Sandra leaned back.

Nick nodded. "Yeah. I have a different question first. Why do you keep looking at your phone? Expecting a call or text to get you out of this so-called date?"

Sandra laughed. "It's not a blind date for sure. We've been friends for several years."

"True. Still, there's got to be a reason you keep looking at your phone. What is it?"

"Well. . .I sorta. . ." Sandra paused. How did she put it? Why did family events require you showing up with someone? Why couldn't the family matchmakers stop trying to match everyone up? They'd made some messed-up choices. She hadn't met anyone she wanted to think about settling down with. Well, almost no one. . .

"I've got something to ask you after you rephrase your first question." Sandra pushed her phone aside. "You go first."

"Okay, How about we go on a real date? One where we spend the weekend together? Act like a couple and see what happens?" Nick crossed his fingers underneath the table. He quickly uncrossed one set of fingers, hoping the old magic adage wasn't correct that two sets could offset each other and cancel out your wish.

Sandra opened her mouth, closed it, and opened it again. "Er. . .*What did you say?*"

"Go on a real date for a weekend and do couple things."

"Where would this be? Why are you asking now?" Sandra gripped the hem of her shirt tightly in her hand.

"Well, Mom and Gram. . ." Nick began.

"Oh crap. They're not friends with my mother, are they?" Sandra clapped her hand over her mouth. She'd blurted out what she was thinking. Great time for her conscience to leave the premises.

"What if they were?" Nick smiled, toying with his napkin.

Sandra arched an eyebrow and squinted at him. He pressed his lips together, hoping to keep his mirth in check. There was no way his parents and Sandra's mother were friends unless Sandra was hiding her magic traits.

"I certainly hope not. My perfectionist and authoritative mother would judge them, size them up and have no qualms about telling them what they thought of your parents based solely on first impressions." Sandra glanced at her phone.

Nick placed his hand palm up middle of the table as he spoke. "Just kidding on that. My mom and gram are snobs too."

Sandra looked up from her phone. "Offering a peace token?"

Nick chuckled. "Yeah, we got a bit off-topic."

"We sure did." Sandra laid her hand palm up close to his. "What's special about your offer?"

"Are you considering it?" Nick placed his napkin on his lap. "Waiter approaches with our appetizers."

Sandra turned, noticing where their waiter was. She smoothed her napkin across her lap. Could she and Nick do, like the cliché said, kill two birds with one stone? Her family reunion was in two weeks. If she didn't show up with a date, her mother was submitting her name to all the online dating services she could find and lining up matchmakers. Her mother's excuse was she loved her and didn't want her to be lonely. Lonely wasn't the issue. Her mother wanted grandbabies. She kept talking about how babies fulfilled womanhood. For her era, yeah. Maybe for some women, it did. Sandra wasn't sure she was ready to consider children. Her job kept her busy and didn't leave a lot of time for dating or kids.

The waiter placed two small plates and two bowls of dipping sauces on the table. Next to the sauce bowls, he set the plates with spring rolls and spicy corn fritters. "Enjoy. I'll be back with your waters in a moment. Your orders are with the chef. I'll let you know when they'll be out when I come back with your waters."

Nick broke open one of the spring rolls, laying it on his plate. "Are you considering my offer?"

Sandra picked up a fritter, blew on it and dipped it in the cheese sauce close to her. "Nick, you never asked me out to just go out beyond our first couple of dates. Why now?"

Nick bit into a piece of spring roll. He chewed and swallowed. Great, was he avoiding answering her?

"You're the best choice." Nick reached for the glass of water the waiter set on the table.

"Excuse me for interrupting. Your meals are a bit delayed. It'll be another ten to fifteen minutes before they're ready." The waiter set the second glass of water in front of Sandra. "Can I get you anything else while you wait?"

" No, thank you. We're fine." Nick drank some of his water and set the glass down. Did he tell Sandra what he needed or wait for her to say what she needed? Damn cat and mouse tactics were a pain in the ass.

"I'm the best choice?" Sandra put her phone in her purse.

"Yeah. I'm considering settling down. You topped the list in a lot of things. Most important is you know me. Most women I know aren't ready to settle down. Are you still sowing your wild oats to quote Gram?"

TWO

"What if I said I was? I mean, it's really none of your business unless I take you up on your offer." Sandra broke the fritter in half and ate one part.

Nick held up three fingers. "First, Leeana said you weren't seeing anyone. You're too busy with work. So I'm not competing with anyone else. Second, when we did go out together, you said you had a good time."

"I did. We agreed that our attraction wasn't the kind that went beyond making the sheets sizzle. So friends were our best option." Sandra popped the second half of the fritter into her mouth.

Nick nodded. "Third, you know me well enough to help me pull off a fake relationship."

Sandra grabbed her water glass, gulped two swallows and clutched the glass with both hands. She slowly set the glass down. *"A fake relationship?"*

"A relationship. Well, an engagement. . ." Nick stopped speaking, his voice trailed off.

Sandra let go of her glass. She placed both hands on the table, leaning forward. "You've got to be kidding."

"Wish I was. Remember I said I needed a favor?" Nick bit into the remaining half of his spring roll. He chewed and swallowed.

"Yeah, and a fake engagement is that favor?" Sandra picked up a spring roll. "You can't find someone who's willing to be your fiancee?"

"I wish there was someone. See, there's something you don't know about my family." Nick leaned forward, closing the space between them as best he could.

"And I'm supposed to go along with this after you tell me this?" Sandra bit off part of the spring roll. Had someone spiked her water? Was Nick joking with her? Frack, the hair on the back of her neck was sticking up, and her stomach kicking like a ready-to-bust loose bucking bronco.

"Hear me out, please."

Sandra slowly exhaled. She hadn't told Nick about the favor she needed. If she didn't hear him out, he might tell her no and walk away. "Okay, explain."

"My family are hybrid shapeshifter magics." Nick stared at her like he expected her to scream or pull away.

Sandra shook her head. "That's normal for Cauldron Falls."

"It is if your whole family is similar. Mine isn't."

"How so?"

"To quote Gram and Mom, I'm one of them. The whispered word—a mortal. Can't shift. No magic. And to further tick the whole lot off, I don't care. I'm tired of being treated as an outlier."

"And I'm supposed to help you fake them out? Not a great place to be amongst shifters and magics. How sure are you we're going to be safe?" Sandra dipped the last fritter in the remaining cheese sauce.

"Pretty damn sure. See, I'm the third male born in this generation. The rest of my cousins and siblings are women. Mom and Gram are hoping I make a match soon to carry on the family name." Nick stacked his plate on top of the empty appetizer plates.

"What about arranged marriages? Aren't those popular with magics and supernaturals?" Sandra added her plate to the stack of plates middle of the table.

"Arranged marriages aren't popular with the liberated women in the family. Matchmaking is extremely popular. Especially Sadie Hawkins full moon matches." Nick scooted to the end of the booth seat, rose and moved closer to her with his hand out.

"I thought we were eating dinner. You change your mind?" Sandra turned partly toward Nick.

"I need to ask you something." Nick reached into his pocket.

"What?" Sandra blinked, trying to make out what Nick had in his hand.

"Yes," Nick began going down on one knee as he opened the box, "Will you do the honor of marrying me?"

Sandra scooted back as far as she could in the booth. There was faking, and there was absurdity. Had Nick gone off the edge?

She glanced down at the petite single solitaire diamond ring the box held. Nick's gaze met hers as she looked up. He smiled. He was serious. Seriously thinking she was going to take his ring as a sign of agreement?

Sandra inhaled, pressed her lips together, knowing her answer might undo her resolve to not end up with a broken heart again. Maybe this time, she could keep her heart out of it.

Yeah, right honey. Unless you're ready to add some stipulations and ones you can abide by too. Great, her conscience finally decided to show back up.

"Yes," Sandra began as Nick leaned toward her, reaching for her hand. "With stipulations. You don't agree; the answer is no."

Nick pulled back. Sandra had stipulations? Shit, it wasn't like they were actually engaged. Yeah, he'd popped the question, even offered up a ring. They both knew it wasn't a real proposal, right?

"Stipulations?' Nick started closing the ring box.

"Yes, stipulations." Sandra laid her hand on his shoulder. "First one is no unprotected sex."

Nick ducked his head, hoping he hid his grin. He hadn't planned on unprotected sex either. He planned on protected sex. Quite a bit of it if Sandra agreed. His and Sandra's sexual chemistry never smoldered when the mood hit them. He looked up. "All right."

"Yes, neither of us needs an unplanned pregnancy. Forced into marriage for real." Sandra held up two fingers. "Second, no bs about me being magical or some percentage shifter. I am not going to try faking that along with everything else."

Nick nodded. "That one I solidly agree with. If we're going to do this, we've got to stick with our story. We've known each other for a while and finally realized we matched."

Sandra flipped up her third finger. "Third stipulation is we keep shit simple. Your family doesn't need to know everything. Neither does mine."

Nick shook his head and pulled back even more. "Your family?"

Sandra flashed him a weak smile and nodded. "Yeah, that favor I need, well, it's not quite as complicated as yours. I need a date for my blasted family reunion, or Mother is going to start her attempts at matchmaking again."

Nick groaned. "Lord, I hope she realizes she can say all the incantations she wants. It doesn't mean she is doing magic."

Sandra chortled, leaning toward him. "Hope springs eternal with her. I let her keep hoping with the magic stuff. I checked with my college roommate, Ariel. Ariel told her no incantations without her approval. Basic old Latin grade school phrases—Hi, my name is, how are you—no issues there."

Sandra held out her hand to him. "I'm asking you to help me fake the engagement for a while longer until my family reunion."

Nick stood. "When is your reunion?"

"Two weeks from now." Sandra reached for the ring box with her other hand.

"*Two weeks?!*" Nick dropped the ring box on the table. "You expect us to fake this for two weeks?"

"When is your family event? Or is it part of the go-away for the weekend you mentioned?" Sandra laid her hands on the table.

Nick sat down opposite Sandra. He started to reach for the ring box. Sandra covered it with her hands. She was interested. Maybe even intrigued. Take the rest of the week for the two of them to work out their story even more. "Paulina and Jackson's wedding is in two weeks, too. Probably right close to your family reunion. I hoped to give us time to work on our back story and get comfortable around each other again."

"You mean give your family eyefuls of us getting close and sweet with each other, don't you?" Sandra pushed their stacked appetizer plates toward the edge of the table. "Our dinner approaches."

Nick glanced toward the open space of the dining area. Their server, accompanied by another server, approached their table. "Sorry for the delay. Your Mahi Mahi Tacos with beans and rice plus extra pico de gallo and sour cream, sir. Careful; the plate is hot."

The server placed a plate in front of Sandra. "Chicken enchiladas with extra pico de gallo, sour cream and cheese sauce with rice and beans. I'll be back with some chips and salsa."

Nick picked up his fork and knife. "Staying with Mom and Gram is not necessary. That is optional. I want them to believe we're together. It's the unspoken question that will come out. What about kids?"

Sandra pointed at Nick with her knife and fork. "You could say you're sterile. Or got a vasectomy."

Gods, the man had balls, huge full of himself ones. If he thought she was going to lie about kids in their future, he could sit on a cake of ice and freeze his sperm and balls twice over! She'd come close to believing one of her exes wanted kids and was willing to plan for them. He talked a lot and did nothing for follow through. She'd almost agreed to marry him until he admitted he was sterile. Short-term engagement...okay, she could go along with that. Screw at

Mom and Gram's in hopes they'd find out and pester them about grandbabies. . . Nope!

Nick laid his utensils down. "I can see I hit a sore spot. I guess that kids are something we need to discuss after we agree on our fake engagement."

Sandra nodded. "Our sexual attraction is strong. Our chemistry smolders when we're together. I don't want this short-term engagement to get out of hand. How about we tell your mom and gram, as well as my mother, we're undecided about when and how many kids?"

Nick shrugged. "Hopefully, that quiets everyone. Mom and Gram can be pitas about things. They hate vague answers."

"Mine too. My family's learned I will shut up and not answer them if they get too nosey. I hope yours can understand as well."

The server placed the salsa and chips on the table and refilled their water glasses. Each watched the other waiting for the other to say more. As the server walked away, Nick picked up his utensils again. "Here's to good food. An enjoyable engagement. I'll give you the ring after dinner, okay?"

Sandra pressed her lips together. Her stomach growled. Further discussion would have to wait. She needed to eat. Nick hadn't fully agreed to her stipulations. Did he have any?

Nick pushed the ring box to the back of the table close to him. Sandra wasn't making any of this easy. She had a stake in this like he did. Part of him didn't want this to be fake, pretend or short-term. When he'd gone done on his knee, his heart skipped a beat. He'd dreamt about proposing a few times recently. He couldn't make out the woman's face in his dreams. A statement flashed across his field of vision right before he fully woke up and opened his eyes. *You know who she is; ask her. Stop pretending. Your heart doesn't lie.* When had the faking become closer to real and without him realizing it?

Three bites into his last taco, Nick glanced at the ring box again. Why he avoided it as he ate, he didn't know?

Neither of them spoke as they ate. Their eyes met from time to time. Had they smiled because they knew they were ignoring the miniature rock inside the box? Was Sandra serious about saying yes if he agreed to her stipulations? Were her stipulations different from those he thought about as he made his list of potential contenders?

Sandra wiped her mouth and hands with her napkin and laid it on the table. She slid to the edge of the booth, picked up her purse and stood. "I'm going to the restroom. We can talk more when I get back."

Nick watched Sandra walk away. He drank the last of his water, pulled the box to him, and slid to the edge of the booth. His conscience had shut up halfway through the first taco. His stomach quietly gurgled its satisfaction and his heart didn't skip a beat as he took the ring out of the box. When Sandra returned from the restroom, he knew it was time.

Nick stood as Sandra reached the table. He took hold of her hand as she faced him, placing the ring in the palm of her hand. "Sandra Cunningham, I agree to your stipulations. Will you do the honor of marrying me?"

Sandra held up the ring. She looked at him and back down at the ring. Did she think he was teasing? Nick dropped down on one knee, still holding Sandra's other hand. "Please say you'll marry me."

Sandra laid enough money on the table to cover her part of the tab. She stepped back from the table, slipped the ring on her left hand, and faced Nick. "I'll get back to you with an answer in a couple of days."

THREE

Nick creamed and sugared the mug of coffee in front of him. Sandra's parting words were she'd be in touch. Nothing other than her one-word response to his text irritated him. Was she having second thoughts?

"Thanks for meeting me for breakfast." Garrett sat on the stool next to him. "Where you been for the last three days?"

"Taking time off. Sandra asked for a few days to think things over. I've been doing the same thing." Nick sipped his coffee.

"Why didn't you tell me you were actually proposing?"

"Actually proposing?" Nick slowly faced Garrett. "What the hell are you talking about?"

"Your proposal lit up Cauldron Falls' social media channels more than the latest Sadie Hawkins Full Moon matches." Garrett saluted Nick with his coffee mug. "How's it feel being Cauldron Falls' latest social media star?"

"Damn it, Garrett. I don't know what you're talking about." Nick leaned closer. "Spill it. I'm not in the mood for a fight."

Garrett sipped his coffee and nodded. "Sorry, bro. I didn't know you were out of the loop. Someone filmed you going down on one knee and proposing to Sandra. I didn't think you were serious about it. You know faking it, not making a real deal out of it."

"Frack! I did it for effect. If Mom and Gram asked when and where I proposed, Sandra had a truthful answer." Nick sipped more of his coffee and set his mug down. "Part of me wants to figure out who filmed and posted it. The restaurant was full and busy."

Garrett laid his hand on Nick's arm. "I hope your mom and gram aren't social media addicts."

Nick laughed. "Flip cell phones are as close to digital as they get unless my uncle convinced them to get tablets or computers."

Garrett grinned. "Electronics. The bane of the magics. Won't work within their magical range and will only work if magic is turned off."

"Learning how to do that is like teaching a mortal to be magical. Strange, different and definitely a foreign language." Nick picked up his utensils as the waitress placed their breakfast special orders in front of him and Garrett. "All right. This proposal has hit the gossip waves. I hope Sandra knows what's going on."

Sandra picked up her cell phone. Who was texting her now? Her phone had blown up with texts from several friends and distant cousins. She'd turned the phone off after the tenth text message around one in the morning. REM sleep captured her shortly afterward. She'd forgotten to set her alarm. Not a problem, except she needed to do laundry, run to the market and figure out how she felt about Nick's proposal.

She looked down at her hand. The ring on her left hand said more than if she spoke aloud. She'd accepted Nick's unique proposal. Accepted his ring, his offer and—he'd pretty much accepted hers. Two weeks of faking—playing make-believe is the word she'd preferred. Part of her wondered if either of them could walk away from this when the two weeks were up.

Nick had recaptured her attention the moment he'd entered Milligans three years earlier. His auburn hair, romanesque jaw and brown eyes drew her in deeper after Leanna and Jackson reintroduced them. Avoiding matchmakers, a full moon and the crowd at Sadie's topped each of their lists that night. Two hours into the evening, Nick asked her to dance. Another hour later, he asked her out. Six months of fun, getting closer and shared emotional and physical intimacy brought them to a fevered pitch. She'd been sure Nick was going to propose then. Sure he was the one until he called, apologizing he couldn't make their date. He was on his way out of town. The phone call cut out before he could say more. She'd caught the boarding announcement before the line went dead. Nick hadn't reached out to reconnect until three years later.

This morning's paper's front page of the arts and entertainment section soaked up her spilled coffee. Nick Morgan, country rock's newest heartthrob, concert dates and interview caught her attention. Goddess, she was engaged to a . . .her mother's designated ring tone sounded.

"Hi, Mom." Sandra held the phone away from her ear. If she put her mother on speaker, the echo would give her away. Maybe she could keep her mother's need to chatter short.

"Sandra, why haven't you called me?"

Why hadn't she called her mother? There was nothing new to tell her. Certainly nothing about the ring on her finger or Nick. That would come closer to time for the family reunion. She slowly put the phone back to her ear. "I've been busy."

"Yes, you have. It's all over social media. My hairdresser told me, your grandmother called saying your cousins told her, and everyone is asking why I didn't tell them about *your engagement to superstar Nick Morgan.*"

Sandra gripped her phone tighter. "What are you talking about?"

"Sandra, don't bullshit me! I'm your mother. It's all over social media and every paparazzi website. The video could be clearer. My future son-in-law shows promise. He proposed the old fashion way."

Sandra pressed her lips together. What the hell had Nick done without telling her?

"Well, mom, we wanted to break the news to you in person. I need to go. I'll call you back." Sandra ended the call.

She tried to call Nick. His voice mail answered. Her phone buzzed twice. Her mother tried calling back. How much time did they have? More like, did she have? Last thing she needed was family descending upon her. Neither did Nick. How much did his family know?

Nick shoved his phone away from him. Mom and Gram wouldn't stop calling. Mom refused to believe him. Gram laughed every time he said, "Yes, I'm engaged. No, she's not pregnant." Deities above, what was it about grandkids? His mom kept asking when and how many. Gram asked almost the same thing. Faking an engagement was easy. A pregnancy? Hell no! That wasn't an option.

He stood, running his hands through his hair as he exhaled. All of this since he'd gotten home. His phone buzzed again.

Nick picked up the phone. What if he let everything go to voice mail? Call back if he felt like it? He glanced at the caller id. "Ah, crap. Not you too, Lenny!" Third call from his agent.

His cell phone vibrated again, followed by a distinctive ringtone. Nick slowly inhaled as the phone vibrated again. Sandra. . .was she calling to cuss him out? How much did she know?

On the third ring, he touched answer, holding the phone away from his ear as he answered. "Hi, Sandra."

A frustrated sigh flowed out of the phone. He clenched the phone tighter. How pissed off was she?

"Why didn't you tell me?"

Nick swiped his sweaty palm on his jeans. Tell her what? Admit he only learned about it this morning? After dodging the paparazzi following him and Garrett as they left the breakfast shop, the last thing on his mind was calling anyone.

"Tell you what?" Nick frowned, knowing he sounded like he was avoiding the herd of elephants in both of their places.

Sandra laid the phone on the table, touched the speaker button, and rose. Pacing hadn't lessened her angst. Shredding junk mail hadn't either. Every time she opened her door, cameras flashed. People rushed toward her with microphones and tape recorders. She couldn't even go out to pick up the morning paper off her front walk without someone snapping a picture. Her duplex neighbor had to sneak out his back door and climb over the low alleyway fence to escape the idiots camped out on her front lawn. And Nick's reply was, *'Tell you what?'*

She dropped back into her chair, drumming her fingers on the kitchen table as she spoke. "About your adoring female fan club...your groupies. . .and your fame and success!"

"Oh, that." Nick's weak chuckle inched her anger temperature three degrees higher. "Uhm—I'm sorry?"

Sandra pressed each tip of her fingers tightly against the table. Counting wouldn't erase the boiling steam welling up inside her. "Nick," she began, pushing back from the table. "There are a dozen or more reporters and people with cameras parked out on my front lawn. My neighbor had to shinny his back fence to escape them."

"Ah shit, Sandra. Damn paparazzi." Nick's long, annoyed sigh flowed out of the phone speaker. "Seriously, I'm sorry."

"How long does this continue?" Sandra paced back to the table and sat back down. "They followed me to the market. Then the pharmacy. Followed me inside and snapped a picture of me talking with one of the clerks I know. She was restocking pregnancy test kits. Three of those paparazzi asses asked me if I knew who the father was as I exited the pharmacy. I didn't buy a damn pregnancy test! I got premenstrual cramps. PMSing with these idiots fucking with me doesn't endear me to them!"

Nick grimaced again. He swallowed twice, shook his head and said, "They're following me around since the damn video hit the social media sites."

"*How long have you known about this?*" There was no mistaking Sandra's ire. Her tone and emphasis said it all.

"Since this morning. No sooner. Let me explain, please." Nick dropped onto his couch. He wasn't going to try to calm Sandra down. Damn video dragged both of them into the middle of a celebrity maelstrom. Groupies, fanatics, and paparazzi loved to blow things out of proportion. Spread rumors, make up vivacious tales, and outrageous lies. A *few* sprinkled liberal bits of truth in amongst their reports. Keyword *few*.

"I'm listening." Sandra's flat tone signaled she'd shifted into neutral. How long that would last, he didn't know. He wasn't guessing either.

"My business manager Lenny didn't know about the video until local news and radio stations started calling. He thought it was about my newest single. Not me proposing in a restaurant."

"When were you going to tell me about your *public music career?*"

Nick winced as Sandra spit out music career like it was a bad word. A social naughty. No, he hadn't told her. He planned to after they'd gotten out of town. His good luck streak had snuck out the back door, leaped the fence and never looked back.

"Once we got to a place, we agreed upon for our get-reacquainted weekend." Why were his palms so damn sweaty?

"Nick," Sandra began, her voice trailing off.

"Sandra, before you say no or that you've changed your mind, let me finish."

"*All right.*"

"Does your back fence have a gate? One that isn't in view of the idiots camped out in your front yard?"

"Possibly. Why?"

"I can send my cousin Victor over to sneak you out the back alley. We can go to a mutually agreed upon secluded place to talk things out." He could use all the good luck-inducing magic he could drum up for a non-magical.

"How can you be sure somebody won't recognize Victor?"

"He's clean-shaven and has a business haircut now. He finished his Ph.D. six months ago. He's teaching at Cauldron Falls University. Nobody's going to recognize him."

Sandra's sigh vibrated the phone speaker. Nick uncrossed his fingers, rolled his eyes heavenward and mouthed a quick prayer. *Come on deities, please let Sandra say yes.*

"If I agree, where would we go?"

"Lenny suggested his cousin's airbnb in Sylvan Valley. It's a small town located about seventy miles from Cauldron Falls. We'll get limited cell phone and internet reception. Only two television stations and the local radio stations are easy listening and local talent. Landline phones are still the rage."

"Sounds pretty secluded. Let me make a couple of calls. I've got to arrange time off and. . ."

Crackling sounded, followed by a loud hum and quiet. Nick looked at his phone. A blank screen. Frack! He'd forgotten to charge the phone thanks to all the ongoing turmoil. Had Sandra said yes without actually saying so?

Nick raced into his bedroom, attached the charger to his phone, and started stripping. He needed to shower, pack and get a text through to Victor. Hopefully, when he got Sandra back on the line, she'd decode her answer. A thought flashed across his mind as he stuffed his dirty clothes in the hamper. Maybe his great-aunt was right. Opportunity arises when things look chaotic. Was this a signal deity heard his prayer, and they were sending signals to use his head for more than a hat rack?

FOUR

Sandra gripped her phone. Last time she snuck out of the house, her mother had grounded her for a month, taken away her car keys, and told her if her grades didn't come up, she'd spend her junior year of high school wishing she'd given her actions more thought. This time sneaking out had to be more covert than disguises. She could slip through the side gate between her and her neighbor Brian's backyards. The hedge between the duplex and the next set of yards blocked any views. If the paparazzi were stupid enough to hop a fence or two, the Anderson's dogs would keep them busy. Brutus and Domingo didn't tolerate trespassers. Brian's sister lived in the duplex next to him, and her Doberman Pincher loved nipping ankles and grabbing pant legs of people he didn't know.

Packing was another issue. She would have to use a backpack to get out of the yard easily. Hopefully, getting into Victor's car would be fast and easy.

Sandra called her boss Cecilia as she trotted up the stairs, two at a time, to her bedroom. Cecilia wasn't going to grant the time off easily.

"Cecilia, you owe me the time off. I took the trip you asked me to cover. I even covered your ass. Dominic wanted the proofs on his desk two days prior to the print deadline. I hand-delivered them three days early. Don't give me shit about wrong time to ask for time off." Sandra put her phone on speaker as she laid it on the bed.

"Sandra, come on. You know we're short-staffed. I need you. Dominic needs you. The magazine needs you. You can't tell me you're taking more time without explaining why. The video of you and Nick Morgan is all over social media. Did he really propose? You gotta give us some inside scoops."

Sandra unzipped her camo-colored backpack and started tossing clothes on the bed. "No, I don't have to give you anything other than I am taking my accrued time off. Talk with HR if you like. I already have. Perhaps we'll talk when I get back."

Sandra ended the call before Cecilia could respond. Copy editor and proofreading jobs came and went. She knew she'd have offers if she decided to freelance. Working for herself might be her best option. More thought along that line would have to wait.

A week away meant packing interchangeable items. Two extra pairs of jeans besides the ones she would wear and five long-sleeved tops filled the bottom of the backpack. A lightweight sweater and windbreaker lay on the bed. Toiletries and undergarments were next. She picked up the hoodie sweatshirt she'd tossed on the bed and a pair of slippers. Depending on the weather, she might need both of them. She put the slippers in an outside pocket and the sweatshirt inside the backpack. The last items she placed on top of her other clothes were a sleep shirt and a lightweight robe.

As she started to strip off her clothes, hoping to grab a shower before she needed to dash out the door, her phone rang. Caller id showed it was Nick. Did she let it go to voice mail?

Sandra grabbed the phone as she headed for the bathroom. "Nick, keep it short. I am. . ." She looked down. She almost blurted out naked and heading to shower.

"Don't worry. I am. Victor is about thirty-five minutes out from your place. Wear your hikers and leather jacket. Oh, yeah. He said put your hair in a ponytail so the helmet goes on easier and quicker. I gotta finish packing. See you soon."

Sandra started to pull the phone away from her ear when Nick blurted out one more thing. "Thanks for going along with this. Love ya for it."

"Wait, you what?" Sandra put the phone back to her ear. Silence. Nick had hung up. *Hung up and said the L word. How dare he?* Fling that word around like it meant. . .she inhaled slowly. There would be time to discuss this when they were face-to-face. She tossed her phone on the counter and stepped into the shower.

As water cascaded over her, she mentally replayed what Nick had said. Hikers? Leather jacket? Helmet? Victor was coming on a motorcycle?

She washed and rinsed as her thoughts continued. Motorcycle fast, quick and—"Loud, noisy and will have the damn paparazzi tailing us. What the hell was Nick thinking?"

Sandra glanced at the bathroom wall clock as she dried. Roughly twenty-five minutes until Victor arrived. She tossed the damp towel over the towel rack, ran a brush through her damp hair and dashed out of the bathroom. Whatever Nick and Victor's plans were, she was part of it. Tossing a neck scarf plus hat and gloves in the backpack quieted her nagging thought that they were heading north into the mountains surrounding Sylvan Valley. Making sure she was dressed and at the back gate ready to go was paramount to getting away and saving what bit of remaining sanity she had.

Fifteen minutes later, she crouched by the back gate listening. Her damp hair hung in a loose braid. The mid-morning sun beat down on her leather jacket. She cracked open the gate, glanced at her watch, and let go a deep sigh. Two gulps of cold coffee and a cereal bar weren't much breakfast. She managed to double knot her hikers and make one last potty stop before she dashed out the door. Her backpack banged against her back as she looked up and down the alley. She squinted. Shook her head and pushed her sunglasses up. Two yards down, a man walking toward her waved. If it was Victor, stealth mode might be their key to successfully escaping.

"Hi Sandra," Victor said, pushing up the visor on his helmet. He held out a similar helmet to her. "Nick said you've ridden before. You ready to ditch the pains?"

Sandra gripped the helmet with two hands. "Yeah. I am more than ready. Once you start the bike, they're going to know."

Victor grinned, shaking his head. "The bike is in the parking lot behind the gas station. We start the bike there."

Sandra smiled. "That's devious and what we need to do. Let's get going." She put the helmet on, tightened the straps and locked the gate.

Ten minutes later, they exited the alley and sprinted across the parking lot to where the bike was parked. Double-checking for followers and finding none, Victor started the bike, steadying it as Sandra got on behind him.

Victor took a quick look around, nodded and pushed the bike forward. "Don't be afraid of putting your arms around my waist and hanging on tight. Nick will meet us at my place twenty minutes from here." Sandra gave two thumbs up. Escaping ignited a sense of adventure. How would it turn out? She didn't bother suppressing her urge to look as they pulled up to the stop sign at the intersection of her street and the main drag. Groups of people milled close to her front yard. What were the flashing lights? She grinned as Victor put the motorcycle into gear. She caught a glimpse of three cop cars with several police standing nearby. Cauldron Falls' finest tolerance for nuisances and idiots, aka looky-loos, was low. Her neighbors were handling the issue. Brian would find her well-placed note taped to his inside back door. She hoped Nick was ready to continue escaping by the time she and Victor arrived.

Nick looked at the clothes he'd hastily stuffed in his duffel bag before driving to Victor's. Two items stood out amongst the clothes. The box of condoms he'd spent ten minutes contemplating taking and a cookbook. Better prepared than not. Thank deity his mom couldn't see his packing. Her 'But Nick babies are an important part of marriage and family' would remain unsaid and unheard like all the other times she blurted it out. Even Gram told her that begging for grandkids didn't get them made.

He chuckled as he stuffed the last of his clothes in the duffel. Neatly folded, ironed and starched with creases his jeans weren't. Three pairs, including the ones he wore, would be enough to get them through the week-long stay. Underwear and t-shirts, his favorite cartoon graphic sweatshirt, and other t-shirts bulged the duffel. If he wasn't running behind, he'd pack neater. Touring had taught him that. Running for planes and long bus rides meant quick and easy packing. Hopefully, his manager's cousin's ranch bunkhouse airbnb had a washer and dryer. The kitchen was supposed to be fully stocked when they arrived. Lenny's chuckle and snicker about bunkbeds ignited weird daydreams filled with him and Sandra trying to get comfortable in a cramped bottom bunk.

Nick chuckled as he stuffed the cookbook into the duffel's side pocket. One of them had to be able to cook. They were supposed to be alone. No public knowledge of their whereabouts or the possibility of PR leaks. Why wouldn't the hair on the back of his neck and his stomach stop jittering every time he thought about Sandra and him alone?

Dude, stop bsing yourself. You got it bad for her. You have for some time. His psyche could shut up.

You don't want me to. You know your heart is in this. You're past caring what your family thinks about mortals. You know you're worth catching and Sandra's the one.

Nick thought about sticking his fingers in his ears and singing 'La-la-la' over and over drowning out— *You can't drown me out. I am you. Stop kicking yourself and get ready to take your chosen lady away.*

Nick sighed as he trotted toward the bathroom. Shower and dress. One good thing he learned during his short stint in the military. Five-minute showers equaled stepping into the shower, soap while under the spray, and rinse. There was something to be said for short hair. Towel dry body and hair. Then pull on his travel clothes.

Ten minutes later, he zipped his duffel closed after tossing in the wool ski cap and gloves Victor had given him. Sylvan Valley's latest weather report called for frost, possible light snow and temperatures in the upper to mid-twenties overnight. Worrying about warmth was the last thing Nick hoped they didn't have to deal with. Shared body heat, especially at night, would alleviate part of the problem.

Now you're thinking. Nice illustration too. His male ego and psyche could shut up. He didn't need Sandra noticing his hard-on tenting his jeans as she came through the door. His ego and heart were in this deeper and stronger than he imagined or anticipated. Could he continue faking what a part of him longed for? What would Sandra say if he told her the proposal wasn't fake? Could he walk away when they were done with Paulina and Jackson's wedding and her family reunion? Would their friendship remain intact if either of them walked away?

FIVE

Victor slowed as he made a right-hand turn into his housing complex. Taking the backway had given them the time he needed to stop for takeout. One of the bike's saddlebags held a large takeout container of coffee, a sack of sweet rolls, three sausage egg and cheese croissants and three bottles of orange juice. The other held the four books he'd run into the local bookstore to grab for Sandra and Nick.

Covert errands were fun until one of his students recognized him. Josh Crandall wasn't known for his quietness. He talked loud and spoke louder if he thought you were ignoring him. Victor told Josh he was taking a few days off. He would see him for class later in the week. Good thing the bike and Sandra were waiting for him in the side parking lot.

Victor pulled into the driveway of the last house in the cul-de-sac. He shut the bike off and dismounted. He raised his visor as he faced Sandra. "Nick is in the house. I'm going to open the garage and put the bike inside. You come on in the garage with me. We'll go in once I shut the garage door."

Sandra nodded, getting off the bike. "How are we going to escape? I don't see Nick's car."

"Exactly. Nick's car would be recognized. It's around back of the garage." Victor pushed the code to open the garage door. "Escaping uses my camper van. I'll explain once we're inside."

Five minutes later, Sandra handed Victor her helmet as the garage door clanged shut. "Thanks for helping me escape this far."

Victor took the takeout bags from her. "Glad to do it. All my years as a roadie taught me one thing, paparazzi are a major pain in the posterior. I worked for upcoming bands. Fame draws people and groupies like a flame draws moths and bugs."

"Didn't know you worked as a roadie." Sandra swung her backpack off one shoulder. She clutched the bag holding the books in her other hand.

"Yes, for about four years. Summers and fall were the best times to be on the road." Victor unlocked the door to the house. "After while, you want a place to call your own. Welcome to my home."

"Thank you, Victor. I understand about a place of your own. My job requires I travel a lot. After a couple of weeks away, you want your own stuff around you and your creature comforts." Sandra followed Victor into the house.

"Hey, Nick," Victor called out, setting the bags he carried on the counter. "We're here. I got takeout from Taters and Eggs. Let's eat."

"Be right there," Nicked called out.

Victor pulled out a chair from the kitchen table. "Sandra, sit down. I'll reheat the food and coffee."

Sandra set her backpack and bag of books on the floor. "What can I help you with?"

"There's plates and mugs in the cabinet to the left of the sink. Silverware is in the drawer same side." Victor placed the takeout coffee container in the microwave and turned it on. "Thanks for your help. Appreciate it."

Nick reached for his duffel bag as his phone rang. Caller id showed Lenny's number. Great, what did Lenny want now? "Hey, Lenny. What's up?"

"I still haven't reached my cousin Agnes. I've made reservations for you at the local hotel as a backup."

"Lenny, the hotel won't work. No privacy. We're out in the open."

"Nick, you and Sandra let me worry about privacy and covert arrivals. You text me when you're on your way."

"Will do. Thanks, Lenny."

Nick ended the call. He put his cell phone in his jeans pocket and grabbed his duffel bag. One thought kept coming to mind as he made his way down the stairs. Finding their own backup place to stay might be a smart idea given Lenny's tone.

The timer on the microwave sounded as Nick entered the kitchen. Sandra saluted him with her mug. "Coffee is hot. Fill a mug and sit down. Croissants and sweet rolls are warm. Orange juice is chilled if you want some."

Nick set his duffel next to her backpack. "Sounds good. My manager Lenny called. He's working on getting us his cousin's airbnb for the week."

"We *don't* have a place to stay?" Sandra set her mug down.

"We do at the local hotel. I told Lenny we weren't ducking and dodging any more paparazzi." Nick filled his mug with coffee and set it next to the orange juice he'd placed on the table.

Victor set three plates on the table. Each held a ham, egg, and cheese croissant and two warm sweet rolls. "I got your place to stay under control."

"Are you sure?" Nick bit into his croissant and chewed.

"Sure am. I've got the bike. The van's got half a tank of gas. It's set up for camping." Victor sipped his coffee and ate more of his sweet roll.

"*Camping?*" Sandra sat upright. "Please tell me we're not roughing it. I'll take ducking and dodging paparazzi over sleeping on the ground in a tent!"

Victor covered his mouth with one hand as he set his mug down. He hastily wiped his hand and mouth. "No tent. The van is a redone camper van. You got a full propane tank, compact bathroom, and sleeps four if you don't mind climbing in and out of the hammock bunk."

Nick stood. "Victor, what about cooking?"

"Two burner induction stove, small combo oven and microwave, fridge operate off the solar power panels if you don't find electrical hook up. Sink tank holds five gallons of water. Bathroom tank ten. Look Nick, you are going to be off the grid living ready if needed. Who is going to be looking for you doing that?" Victor handed Nick his plate. Nick put their plates in the sink.

"No one. Not even me. I guess it's better than dealing with paparazzi. Private and secluded for sure if we can find a campground." Nick faced Sandra, holding out his hand. "It's not a tent. We may still luck out with the airbnb. Backup plans are better than winging it."

Sandra slowly exhaled. Escaping wasn't going to be simple and easy. No, it was turning into a topsy-turvy adventure that had a bunch of twists and turns. "Okay, yeah, it's better than a tent or dealing with more damn paparazzi. Let's check the van out and make sure we got basics. I don't want to have to make a dash and shop trip before we get out of Cauldron Falls."

Victor opened the door to the garage. "There's plenty of canned goods. You can raid my freezer and fridge while I get you sheets, blankets and pillows."

"Do you do much cooking?" Nick opened the fridge.

"Depends on what you call cooking. Do you?" Sandra opened the side-by-side freezer next to the fridge.

"I'm sure we can open a can and heat up the contents. Reminds me, best grab a couple of pans and lids too. Maybe a skillet and lid. I packed a cookbook just in case." Nick placed a loaf of bread on the table along with a container of butter.

"*Look, I can read a recipe.*" Sandra dropped two packages of lunch meat on the table. Their thud echoed off the kitchen walls.

"I can too. I misspoke. I apologize." Nick pulled two plastic grocery bags from the large grocery bag storage bin on the wall. He held one out to Sandra. "One of us is going to have to do the cooking or meal coordinating."

"*We* can *both* pitch in. I think we need to inventory the camper before we get much more." Sandra placed the frozen food in the bag.

"Agreed." Nick took hold of her hand. "We can see what there is and fill in. Sylvan Valley is rural without a major grocery chain. Country living is what we're getting."

*Great. . .*her last time in the country was her twelfth birthday. Her cousin's brother harassed the bull they were boarding until he treed them after chasing them around the pasture. If this escape morphed anymore, they'd be stuck in the camper deities might know where.

"Here's two sheets, two pillows and extra blankets. There's a double sleeping bag in the camper that you can use as an extra layer if it gets cold or chilly. The hanging bunk only needs sheets and a blanket. The dinette folds out into a queen size bed too." Victor placed the large trash bag containing the sheets, blankets and pillows near the door.

The next several moments were spent inventorying the canned goods in the camper. Soups, chili, and oatmeal, along with other canned goods gave Sandra several ideas for quick, easy meals. She'd test Nick's cooking prowess as needed. Packed a cooking book indeed!

Forty minutes later, Victor pulled out in Nick's car, waved as he turned, heading into Cauldron Falls. Hiding the car at their cousin Tony's garage might throw the paparazzi off long enough to let Nick and her escape. Nick glanced at her as they entered the highway. Five hours to Sylvan Valley. Five hours of back roads and deity knew what. Sandra hoped Victor was right that his GPS was up to date on the major back roads leading to the two-lane mountain pass entering Sylvan Valley.

Wednesday Evening-Five hours later

Nick glanced at Sandra. She sat rigidly in the passenger seat since Lenny's call. Nick didn't blame her for being miffed. Lenny couldn't reach his cousin. No one knew if her airbnb was available. Lenny's hotel backup fell through due to a power outage and broken water pipes. That left them two options try and find a room at the local bed and breakfast if it was open. They were at the tail end of their season. The other—Horseshoe Bend campgrounds—thrilled him as much as it did Sandra. . . not thrilling at all.

"I know it's not what we planned on." Nick pulled into the first parking space close to the campground office.

Sandra's sarcastic laugh made him shiver. She glanced at him as she spoke. "Planned on? We did getting the food together. The bedding and even grabbing bath soap and shampoo at the quick mart when we stopped for gas. We knew we were going to end up camping."

"Yeah, we did. Didn't want to admit we'd probably end up here. I swear Lenny and Victor planned this." Nick shut off the motor.

"Don't blame Victor. At least he made sure we got away. We're fine for the next several days. He even fielded that call from his mom when she called trying to get info out of him to pass on to your mom." Sandra slouched down in the seat.

Nick held out his hand. "Peace? I really prefer it instead of us snapping at each other and breaking the peace."

Sandra snorted. "Our spats have never been long. We blow up, say what we're feeling and cool off. Sure. Peace." She laid her hand on his.

Nick slowly inhaled and exhaled. If Lenny and Victor were in on this, they'd have a lot of explaining to do. A hell of a lot. "All right, let's find out what space we set up in for the next few days."

Sandra grabbed her fanny pack off the floor as she opened the passenger side door. "We're here until Brian calls or we go to your cousin's wedding."

"Brian calls?" Nick pressed his lips together, hoping the rest of his retort died before he blurted it out. Who the hell was Brian? Had Sandra bullshitted him on not seeing someone?

"You're turning red, Nick. Calm down. Brian is my neighbor. I'm not a two-timer." Sandra exited the van.

Nick grabbed the rearview mirror and turned it toward him. Red tinged his forehead and cheeks. Deity on high, was he that damn easy to read? He couldn't keep his emotions under control?

Dude, who you trying to fool? She gets to you more than you want to admit. Maybe you need to listen to your heart. We been trying to tell you for a while. When are you going to hear what we've got to say?

Great, his conscience had tossed its lit match and gasoline onto the smoldering inferno he was trying to control. Nick gripped the steering wheel tighter. A week ago, his heart wasn't in this. Now it was?

SIX

Nick let go of the steering wheel, opened the driver's door and got out. Sandra had come to him ready to ask for a favor. He'd done the same. They needed each other in unique ways. One thing kept coming back to him when he first heard Garrett's suggestion, trust was important. Whoever he chose to go through with this, he needed to trust. Did Sandra feel the same way? Was their trust strong enough to withstand the media blitz, his family and hers?

Sandra fastened her fanny pack around her waist. She looked up at the clouds gathering north of the pass they'd driven through. Cool temps and frost on the peaks were what the gas station attendant had mentioned. The evening sun began its descent as they entered Sylvan Valley. The town reminded her of the small coastal village pictures her grandmother had hung on her wall. Rural, laidback, and. . .quiet. Everyone they'd met took time to talk with them, introduce themselves and ask why she and Nick were in town. A few mentioned little to no cell phone reception. Local radio stations played classical and easy-listening music. Television stations shut down at midnight. It was like they'd entered another time and place. Someone asked if they were attending the local Sadie Hawkins full-moon festivities in a few days.

"Nick," Sandra began as she made her way around the front of the van. "It's tranquil and peaceful. No loud roar of traffic or the constant hum of white noise. I've heard birds chirping, felt the wind blow across my face and even caught the fragrance of the flowers blooming outside the gas station and restaurant."

"Yeah, Sylvan Valley is off the main road. Small town living like when our grandparents and parents were coming up. I sorta stopped worrying about hiding out. Not like someone is going to surprise us here." Nick shut the driver's side door.

"No surprises needed. Let's see what spots are available. I hope close to the pool house is open. Plenty of hot water available." Sandra started up the front office steps.

"Hang on for a minute." Nick moved up beside her. "Okay, if asked, we say we're engaged? We're engaged unofficially and officially if you count social media."

Sandra looked down, pressed her fingers against her legs, and rubbed her lips together. Nick was right; they were officially engaged thanks to the paparazzi. Nothing said they couldn't call it off later. Fake it for the time being. Fulfill their mutual agreement. She looked up. Nick winked, grinning as he nodded toward the office.

Nick leaned closer, whispering. "Someone is watching us through the window. We can practice and iron out the rough spots before we meet Mom and Gram and your family. What do you say?"

Sandra reached for Nick's hand. "Sure. Nothing says we have to tell a tale. We're taking a few days away from our jobs."

"What are our jobs?" Nick entwined his hand with hers.

"I freelance as a copy editor and proofreader. I have my own business. You?"

Nick grinned and nodded. "How about I write songs?"

"Partially true, I suspect." Sandra closed the space between them and whispered. "Hopefully, they don't ask you to sing any."

Nick chuckled. "I did bring my guitar."

"Maybe we're saved, or is it we're safe?" Sandra brushed her lips across Nick's and pulled back.

"Come on, sweetie. Let's go find out where we're camping for the next few days." Nick let go of her hand and bounded up the steps.

Sandra shoved her sweaty palm inside her jacket pocket. Sparks of warmth had swarmed over her hand and partway up her wrist as Nick pressed his palm tighter to hers. Magic wasn't supposed to be involved, or was it?

Nick glanced at his hand, turning it over twice. Nothing unusual. What had just happened? Heat had seared its way across his palm, edged up his wrist and lingered close to his pulse point. Sandra wasn't a magic. Victor's magic traits weren't love spell-focused. Victor shapeshifted with ease, used moonlight to ignite fires and starlight to navigate by. Sailors of old natural magic mixed with animal magic. A rare talent that included some of the family said the beguiling lure of the sea sirens' musical abilities. Victor had a damn near pitch-perfect ear when it came to tuning instruments. His love of science grabbed his heart from the moment he got his first potion right.

Nick turned and faced Sandra. "Problem?"

Sandra shook her head as she moved up the steps. "No. Thinking about what *we're* going to do about dinner."

"Cook and eat it, I guess." Nick grinned. "I grabbed a couple boxes of microwave fries when we stopped for gas at the convenience store. How about a grilled cheese sandwich with shredded cheddar and gouda cheese and fries?"

"You snuck the good cheese out of Victor's fridge?" Sandra laughed.

"Yup. Figured if Victor fussed about it that much, we were worth it. 'Sides he had more in the freezer. He'll cuss and fuss a bit. I'll get him more when we get back to Cauldron Falls." Nick opened the office door.

Sandra stepped up beside him and whispered, "Dinner is sounding good. I hope you cook as good as you meal plan."

She moved past him on into the office. Nick raised his hand to his chin, sure his mouth hung open. Score five Sandra! She just laid dinner prep and cooking on him. There was still dishwashing and bedmaking. Shared warmth with the pending forecast of possible frost down in the valley might not be a bad idea. He wondered how much room a zipped-close double sleeping bag provided.

"Good evening. Welcome to Horseshoe Campgrounds." A slender older dark haired woman moved out from behind the counter. "I'm Wanda. My husband Hal and I own the campgrounds."

"Nice to meet you, Wanda." Sandra nudged Nick as she moved forward, holding her handout.

Nick flashed a quick sideways glance at Sandra as he spoke. "Glad to meet you, Wanda."

"Kinda late in the year for camping." Wanda flipped open the registration book on top of the counter. "Most folks packed up weeks ago and headed out of the valley except us local residents."

"Some of us can't get away during peak vacation times." Sandra grasped Wanda's hand briefly and let go.

"Yeah," Nick said, reaching the counter. "We figured get away before the snow falls."

Wanda laughed. "Peaks are getting frost and a spattering of that white stuff. Nothing that will linger long once the sun comes up tomorrow. You folks here for the Sadie Hawkins Festival?"

"Sadie Hawkins?" Sandra picked up the pen next to the registration book.

"Yes, full moon Thursday night. Local matchmaker helps couples match up. Joining ceremonies are performed around the community center bonfire. Local talent entertains. You can bring a dish for the community potluck." Wanda turned the registration book toward Sandra.

"Who do we let know if we're interested?' Sandra signed the register.

Wanda spun the register back around, leaned down, squinting. "Sandra, right?"

Sandra nodded.

"You can tell me by noon tomorrow. Hal and I provide two of the main dishes. Ralph, our main chef, prepares a couple of side dishes and a dessert or two. " Wanda laid a blank note card on the counter. "Not being nosy, Sandra, but I need to see some id."

Nick grinned and elbowed Sandra as he laid his id on the counter. "I'm Nick. I noticed there's not many cars in the parking lot."

Wanda handed him a pen. "We got a few year-round tenants. Some RVers and most in the few cabins we've got."

"Is a cabin available?" Nick signed the register.

"Sorry. Full up for the Sadie Hawkins Festival Thursday night. You're welcome to use the space close to the pool house. You can back into the spot and hook up to the electric, water and sewer for free."

"Thanks. How much for a week?" Nick reached for his id.

"Usually forty dollars a day. Off-season and not often used space, twenty a day. Hundred for a week." Wanda pulled his id toward her. "Need to make a copy. Yours too, Sandra. Let's us keep up with our patrons."

Nick looked at Sandra. She shrugged, placing her id next to his. "Keep up with your patrons?"

"Be able to say who's here and show pictures if needed. Nothing to worry about unless you're shape shifters. . ." Wanda's voice trailed off.

Sandra looked at Nick. Nick shook his head and shrugged.

"Shape shifters?" Sandra gripped the inside of her jacket pockets tighter. Great, they were the one-outs in a community of magics and supernaturals? How the frack had that happened? She glared at Nick.

"Some citizens get full moon hairy. Woods is thick and off the well-known paths—some have gotten lost and found au natural the next day. Helps to have a photo to compare faces with." Wanda picked up the two copies off the scanner and handed the ids back. "Here ya go. Enjoy your stay."

"Thank you." Nick picked up his id and the numbered plastic tag next to it. "What is this for?"

"Space number. Lets the sheriff and his deputies know you are registered guests." Wanda slid Sandra's id toward her plus a festival flyer.

Sandra pocketed her id. "If we do decide to come, not much room in the camper to cook for twenty-five people."

"You can use our kitchen for baking. Just let me know by Thursday midday.
"

Sandra picked up the flyer and faced Nick. "Sure will. Don't think we need matchmaker appointments. We made our match choice already."

"Sure did, sweetie." Nick held her hand and turned. He whispered as he did. "We could say we're engaged."

Sandra smiled, whispering her reply. "Let's not until it's necessary."

"Thanks again, Wanda," Nick called out as they reached the door. "See you in the morning."

"You're welcome. Have a good evening."

Hal exited the office as Wanda closed the register. "That guy looks familiar. Like Eleanor Morgan's grandson. Did you copy their id?"

Wanda slid the two copies out from under the registration book. "Have you ever known me not to?"

Hal shook his head. "A time or two maybe." Hal pulled the copies to him. "Sure does look like Eleanor Morgan's grandson."

"No, I didn't ask. If it is, he's of age. Still. . . " Wanda stopped talking.

"Still what?" Hal faced her.

"Well, he's with a woman. She's wearing what looks like an engagement ring. Eleanor told her cousin Bethany that Nick got engaged recently. Dang, social media video is too grainy to tell with our internet speed." Wanda pulled the copies out of Hal's hand and shoved them into the needs filing folder on top of the credenza next to the office entrance.

"Quite a few spur-of-the-moment weddings happen each festival." Hal slipped his arm around Wanda's waist. "Who knows, that young couple might be one of them?"

Nick waited until he and Sandra were outside to let go of her hand. "Are you seriously considering attending the festival?"

Sandra faced him as she reached the bottom step. "Possibly. Mingling might be a good cover. We've got our jobs figured out. You can sing a song or two. It's not like we're looking to win anything. Swapping stories should be easy. We tell about meeting up and realizing we meshed. It's not far from the truth."

"And the potluck dish? We don't have enough to feed twenty-five people." Nick got in the driver's side and started the van.

"We do. The brownie and cake mixes we grabbed out of Victor's pantry. Chocolate sauce and melted sugar for frosting. I'm sure I can get four or five eggs from Wanda. A couple sheet pans of frosted cake brownies is plenty." Sandra closed the passenger door.

"You sure you're up for this?" Nick put the van into reverse.

"I can cook. Stretching a cake recipe isn't hard when you're doubling the batch. Brownies and chocolate are most folks' fave. We got to practice faking things. Why not here and now?" Sandra fastened her seatbelt.

SEVEN

Nick swallowed his comeback. He'd hoped for a bit of practice before they'd went public. A few days of wooing Sandra. Some privacy and. . .his gonads needed to cool down 'cuz relief wasn't happening anytime soon. Could he convince Sandra to take some time to work on their passionate PDAs and kissing too?

"How about some dinner?" Nick asked as they approached their campsite.

"Tonight it's simple and easy. sandwiches, chips and cookies." Sandra yawned.

Nick pressed his lips together trying to stifle a yawn. He glanced at his watch. "It's not even eight-thirty. Too early for sleeping."

Sandra patted his shoulder. "We got to set up. Get dinner made and figure out how the dinette converts into a bed. I call dibs on the hammock bunk."

"Figuring things out includes lighting the heater. It's going to take a while before the temperature levels out. I say shared heat is a good idea. Cuddling and sharing the double sleeping bag is probably our best option."

"Really? I think bundling is a better option." Sandra unfastened her seatbelt as he started backing into the space.

"*Bundling? What's that?*" Nick glanced in the side mirror, squinting.

"Rolled blanket down the middle of the bed aka our sleeping area. Think the double sleeping bag has enough room for the three of us—you, the blanket roll, and me? I'm sure you and the wall can figure out your sleeping position. I'm staking out my half before the bundle settles in." Sandra opened her door. "You might want to put a towel or two up against that outside wall. It might not be well insulated."

"Wait," Nick called out, opening his door. "We need to talk."

Sandra came around the backside of the van. "What do you think we're doing? You don't need to yell. Unless you want everyone to know you're snuggling with a cold wall and a rolled-up blanket. Might get you some weird looks and gossip going."

Nick rolled his eyes, glanced over his shoulder and cussed. Pitch-black nightfall darkness greeted him. The more he tried to focus into the growing darkness the more he swore he heard snickers and laughs. He knew no one was out there. He'd shined the lights around the area as he turned around and backed up. His blasted conscience and psyche could stop rolling on the floor laughing their existential asses off, much less peeing their pants if they wore any.

"Come on, Sandra. Seriously, can we please talk about this after dinner?" Nick closed the driver's side door.

Darkness engulfed him four steps down the side of the van. Couldn't see his hand, where the van ended or how far back he needed to go. "Sandra, I need your help."

"Come on, say it a little louder," a voice said behind him. Nick jumped, flinging his hands out, fists clenched.

"You need this." A beam of light arced across his face and down toward the ground. "How long has it been since you roughed it?"

Nick inhaled slowly, several cuss words fought to spew forth. He pressed his lips tighter together. Sandra closed the space between them, shining the flashlight on the ground. "You really don't want me to answer that."

"Oh, I do. You see, this isn't a one-sided situation. I need you to help me out with my family situation. You need me to help you out with yours. And. . ." Sandra paused, counting to five as she did.

"And?" Nick leaned against the van.

"We need each other, Nick. We've got to stop hiding and assuming. Let's get inside, warm up, and fix dinner. We need to get better at partnering with each other." Sandra turned, shining the flashlight out in front of her. "Best come back this way unless you want to deal with bushes and thorns."

"Shit, how did you see them and I didn't?" Nick's breath warmed her neck.

"I came prepared. Mini Mag pen flashlight. When you travel as much as I have, you learn being prepared matters. Blackouts, storms, and caught on the side of the road with a flat tire at dusk aren't things you care to repeat." Sandra reached back for Nick's hand.

"Okay, I owe you. I haven't camped since my teens. Can we get inside and discuss this over food?" Nick's stomach growled loudly, protesting its emptiness.

Sandra sighed. "Come on. The bushes offer some insulation if the storm reaches down into the valley tonight. We need food and warmth."

Nick took her hand. "You lead. I follow. Seems there is a rhythm to this that we are all right with."

"Yeah, I lead, you follow. You bumble, I get us out." Sandra snickered.

"One damn minute," Nick began.

"I'm teasing. We've worked together to get here. Come on we're at the front of the van." Sandra clicked off the flashlight and moved into the dimming beam of the headlights.

"We have. Some of it we had to. I'm too tired and hungry to care who posted the video. Thanks for showing up and taking on this challenge." Nick kissed her cheek.

"You're welcome. I located the electric hook-up cable and where the hook-up is on the outside of the pool house." Sandra clicked on the flashlight as the van's parking lights shut off.

"I'll take care of the hook-up. Flashlight please." Nick held out his hand.

Cussing, fussing and laughter filled the next few moments. Sandra's giggles, Nick's laughter and a few quick kisses delayed getting the interior lights on. A few more moments passed before Nick opened the camper's outside door.

Sandra brushed past him, sliding her hand along the interior wall until she came to the round-handled dimmer switch. She turned the switch until the interior hanging lamp close to the sink glowed, emitting a soft golden light. "Nick, come on in."

Nick climbed in, pulling the door closed behind him. "Light. Next heat. Where did Victor say the panel for the heater is?"

"Halfway down the back wall close to the rear window." Sandra sat on one side of the u-shaped dinette bench.

"Done. Glad we have electricity. Partial heat is better than none." Nick clicked the pilot light panel closed. "Doubt the microwave will work."

Sandra stood and opened the cabinet over the sink. "It may. In the cooler are cold cuts, cheese and bread. We might be able to heat up a couple of sandwiches. There's chips and cookies stashed in here."

Nick lifted the cooler onto the table. "Let's see what we can do. A warm sandwich, chips and cookies sound good. I'm going to get the electric and sewer hooked up. That way we can have a hot drink, water for cleaning up and brushing teeth."

"Okay. I'll get the sandwiches ready." Sandra placed the cooler lid on the dinette table. "Nick, wait a minute."

She turned around as Nick exited the camper. Victor had texted something about the camper's rooftop solar panels right before they pulled out. Sandra pulled her cell phone out of her fanny pack. She scrolled to Victor's last message.

The solar panels are set to store energy as you drive.
Even with the overcast afternoon, you'll have enough
power to cook, heat and lights for a few hours. Safe
drive. The panels will continue to store energy if you
are able to hook up to electricity at the campgrounds.

"I'm back. Hook up is done. Sandwiches ready?" Nick closed the door behind him.

Sandra grabbed a pan out of the box they'd hastily tossed pans and cooking utensils into. She turned the faucet handle closest to her. Water splashed out in between blasts of air. "Lock the doors. We're in for the night."

"Sure," Nick said, turning around. "Do you need help fixing the sandwiches?"

Sandra set the pan on the small induction cooktop and turned it on. "Get the bread and cold cuts out. Water should be hot in a bit. We can microwave the sandwiches as soon as I find the plates."

"Hot water? Microwave?" Nick set the bread and cold cuts on the table.

Sandra nodded, grinning. "Yes. Thanks to Victor."

She handed Nick her cell phone. "Read Victor's text."

Nick glanced down, his lips moving. "We got power, heat and. . .hot damn!"

Sandra laughed. "Well, not that hot. Probably enough to take a rinse down quick shower each from the water tank if we conserve water."

Nick opened his mouth. Sandra clapped her hand over his mouth. "No, that does *not* mean sharing the shower. Besides, not enough room."

Nick kissed the palm of her hand before taking it off his mouth. "Well can't blame me for trying." Nick winked and sat down at the dinette. Could he convince Sandra to help him conserve heat? Two bodies close and a double sleeping bag without that blasted bundle she mentioned between them. . .he looked up. Sandra stared at him, holding out two plates. There'd be time to discuss other conservation ideas after dinner.

"Are you helping? Or gawking?" Sandra set the plates on the table.

"Sorry. Mind elsewhere. Been a long day. Kinda weird I don't have a lot of things going down." Nick pulled the plates to him.

"I get it. I keep thinking I need to keep checking if some idiot is lurking, waiting to snap some asinine photo and write bs about it." Sandra set two mugs on the table. "Herbal tea or hot chocolate?"

"What flavor herbal tea?" Nick put two slices of bread on each plate. "Ham and cheese or turkey and cheese?'

Sandra held up two boxes of tea. "Tea is a mint medley or chamomile. Turkey, ham and cheese, please."

"Do we have sweetener?" Nick set the plates and sandwiches aside.

"Honey. Two bottles. Which tea you want?" Sandra put a tea bag in one mug.

"Whatever you're having. Either one is fine." Nick patted the space next to him. "Sit down for a moment."

Sandra put a tea bag in the other cup and put the boxes away. "Why?"

"I got a question."

Sandra turned away. Last time Nick said that she ended up engaged. What could he want now? They'd escaped. The great getaway had turned into a campout. Last time she'd gone camping with friends. . .no her thoughts weren't going there. Nick had already tried the save water shower with a friend approach.

She turned back and picked up the plate closest to her. "Is this let's conserve heat and share the sleeping bag?"

"Well. . .er.er." Nick looked away.

"Nick, not again, okay? We've got sheets, pillows, and extra blankets plus the sleeping bag. The heater is working." She reached for the other plate. "Only way I am going to share that blasted sleeping bag with you is completely unzipped and like another blanket."

"Come on, Sandra. We've shared a bed before." Nick handed her the plate.

"We have. You aren't expecting the same outcome, are you?" Sandra put one plate in the microwave to warm.

"At some point. . ." Nick stopped talking.

"At some point what?" Sandra filled each mug from the steaming pan and placed it in the sink.

"Never mind. Where's the honey?" Nick slid to the end of the bench.

Sandra closed the space between them. She leaned down and asked, "Is this the friends-with-benefits talk?"

"Ah, yeah, I guess." Nick crossed his arms. "We gotta at some point."

"Gotta what?" Sandra pressed her lips together, trying not to smile.

"Do it. Have sex. Use the condoms." Nick looked away.

"Why?" The microwave timer buzzed. Sandra leaned down. "I've never known you to blush, Nick."

EIGHT

Nick tried to stand. "I'm not blushing. Back up."

"I'll back up. There isn't a lot of room." Sandra moved sideways, creating a small space between them. "If you aren't blushing, why are your cheeks red?"

"Sandra, men don't blush." Nick rose, turning as he tried to move past Sandra.

"Okay. Your cheeks are tinged. Why? You getting sick?" Sandra reached up; her palm turned toward him. "What kind of doctor do I take you to?"

Nick cleared his throat. "A regular one. Just because my gene pool is magical doesn't mean I don't get sick like you do. Remember, I got the mere mortal cursed genes."

Sandra lowered her hand. "Sounds like some interspecies breeding going on."

"Between the shapeshifter genes, the magic ones, and the mortals who joined the clan many generations ago and a few more recent, I wouldn't be surprised if there is." Nick reached for his mug. "Who's sandwich is ready?"

Sandra took the plate out of the microwave. "Yours if you're ready to eat."

"Go ahead and sit down. I can warm mine up. You talked with Victor more about the heater and stuff before we bolted out of his place. Bring me up to speed, okay?"

Sandra placed her plate on the table and sat on the opposite side of the dinette. "The dimmer light switch is on the wall opposite the door we came in. You know where the heater switch is. You did the electrical hook-up."

Nick put his plate in the microwave to warm. "What about the shower and toilet?"

Sandra ducked her head. Nick moved closer. Was she blushing now?

"Ah, Sandra, are you blushing?" Nick pushed her tea mug closer to her.

Sandra looked up. Her pressed tight-together lips formed a lopsided grin. She shook her head. "Not intentionally, I guess. Men usually know all the mechanical aspects and women—we're assumed to not know this stuff."

Nick snorted. "Ain't liberation great. I don't mind you knowing this stuff. It's gonna take both of us working together to get through this week."

"Get through faking our families out too." Sandra tore her sandwich in half. "Before you sit down, the switch for the tankless water heater is on the wall opposite the heater. Victor said it takes about twenty minutes to heat up."

Nick set his mug on the table. "Go ahead and eat. I'll get it."

Sandra rose and opened the cabinet over the cooktop. She laid the bag of chips she took out on the table. She sat down as Nick came back to the table.

"Everything okay?" he asked, sitting down.

"Yes. Got the chips." Sandra picked up her mug, holding it out as she spoke. "Here's to quiet. Getting a good night's sleep and figuring out where we go from here."

"Agreed." Nick touched his mug to hers. "Let's eat."

Sandra bit into her sandwich. Her usual sub sandwich order included banana peppers, a bit of hot relish, and a combination of lettuce, tomato and cilantro. Something with a bit of heat and a kick as her tastebuds encountered each bite. Tonight, buttermilk bread, American cheese plus the ham and turkey without condiments tasted richer and better than any of her creative sub orders. The salt and vinegar chips added zest as she ate two after finishing half her sandwich. Simple fare, easy prep, and good company—Nick wasn't hard on the eyes. He pitched in so far. Her great Aunt Minnie said blessings came without fanfare. Sandra sipped her tea as she leaned back against the seat's cushions. There was a lot to be thankful for and many blessings to count. One of the biggest was the camaraderie she and Nick had going. Every time she reminded herself this was temporary and fake, her heart skipped a beat. Part of her wanted to curl up and cry. Did it have to be fake?

Nick reached for the bag of chips. The few women he'd dated were more interested in his fame than him. Sandra didn't appear infatuated with his fame. What little there was of it. She'd accepted the challenge of escaping the paparazzi, taking a chance on going away with him without concrete plans, and even flexed in making decisions to come here. Could she be the one? The one his great G-maw talked about. The one that made his heart zing. Beat faster when he thought about her. Brought him peace and joy instead of pieces and blips of momentary happiness. His heart had beat a bit faster and—his hormones went zing and hadn't stopped percolating since she agreed to help him out. Accepting what his heart and psyche kept showing and telling him wasn't his usual style. Maybe it was time for a change.

"What you thinking about?" Nick popped a chip in his mouth. Talk about a loaded question. Would Sandra change the subject or say nothing and let his attempt at conversation die?

Sandra looked up. "How quiet it is. How good the food tastes. There's part of me ready to jump up and check for lurkers. My subconscious is still on vigilant mode. What about you?"

Nick nodded. "About the same. I've spent the better part of the last year recording, interviewing and being in the limelight more than expected. The quiet and tranquility feel surreal. I know it's not."

Sandra held up the remaining half of her sandwich. "Back in Cauldron Falls, I'd doctor this up and never think about tasting the sandwich before doing it. Here I like the bite of the chips, the tang of the cheese, and the mix of the ham and turkey."

"Yeah. I think you've hit on something. We're savoring the simple basic things. Taking time to relax and breathe as my great G-maw used to tell me. Rushing through life doesn't mean you get more." Nick wiped his hands and face with his napkin.

"Very true. My family has a long-time belief that deity watches over you and brings you what you need when you least expect it. We need time to talk and plan. Appears we got it." Sandra finished her sandwich as Nick continued talking.

"Do you think we should go to the festival tomorrow?" Nick put his plate and mug in the sink.

"We can talk about that tomorrow. Right now I have something else I think we need to discuss." Sandra handed Nick her plate and mug.

"Okay." Nick faced her. "What is it?"

"Who's showering first? Are you worried about sex happening?"

Nick opened his mouth, closed it and held up his hand. He shook his head and sat down. "Ah—ah hell, I don't know. Does it matter?"

Sandra slowly exhaled. She laid her hand on Nick's arm. "Shower order, no. Sex yes. I'm glad you brought condoms. Thank you. I think we need to sleep tonight. Get rested and see what tomorrow brings."

Nick yawned. "I'll take the hammock bunk."

"No need. Victor said the dinette turns into a queen size bed. Shared warmth is nice on cold nights. I'll get the dishes done while you shower." Sandra reached for the cooler.

"I've got it. You sure about sharing a bed?" Nick placed the cooler back in its storage space and faced her.

Sandra brushed her lips over Nick's. "I trust you. Yes, I'm sure."

Nick stepped back. "You know you turn me on. We got chemistry. I want to be sure you're ok sharing a bed with me."

Sandra refilled the earlier pot with water from the sink and put it on to heat. "Nick, at some point, you gotta trust you. Or are you saying you don't trust me?"

"You don't have to sleep with me here." Nick moved his duffel off the dinette seat.

"Before you say more, sit down and hear me out." Sandra sat down. Nick sat next to her. "I'm too tired to care about intimacy tonight. Sex is not on my mind. A few hugs and snuggles are *all* you're going to get."

Nick slipped an arm around her shoulders and hugged her. "I'm overthinking. I want things to work out. My family to accept us."

Sandra shrugged. "Our families are going to accept us or they aren't. I'm not going to lose sleep over that. I am worried about yours and getting turned into a toad or zapped into another realm. Or chased down by a rabid half shifted whatever."

Nick lowered his arm. "My mom and Gram are stalwart upholders of the second magic law that says no magicing any mortal. One of the reasons I am glad you are with me. Mom and Gram aren't going to be able to matchmake me."

Sandra slid to the end of the bench. "Then why do you need me with you?"

"Did you miss what I said?" Nick rose. "I don't need their constant chatter about getting married and all the available female supernaturals. I like my women mortal and nonmagical like me."

"Can we talk about this tomorrow? I'm beat. You're yawning. Go shower." Sandra squirted dish detergent on the plates and mugs as she poured warm water into the sink.

"Okay. That bathroom is cramped. Gotta sit on the toilet to shower. Be out in five." Nick started undressing.

Sandra looked away, focusing on washing the plates and mugs. Had Nick packed sleep shorts? Or did he still sleep nude like she remembered? She swallowed hard hoping he'd packed sleep shorts even if he preferred to sleep nude. Keeping her psyche off a nude man in bed with her wouldn't be easy.

Nick shucked the last of his clothes outside of the cramped bathroom. He peeked around the door before closing it. Sandra's back was to him. When was the last time they'd seen each other nude? Three years ago? It felt longer. He clicked the door shut and turned the shower on.

"Damn that's cold!" He twisted the shower lever until warm water splashed out of the handheld shower head. Soaping and rinsing weren't going to be easy. His best option was a combination of soaping down and rinsing as best he could sitting and standing.

Ten minutes later, he opened the door, grabbed the towel off the outside knob and wrapped it around his waist. The air blast rushing over him felt warmer than when he stripped down. Good sign the heater was working.

Nick stepped out of the bathroom, glanced toward the front of the camper and grinned. An awesome view of Sandra's pert ass greeted him as she bent over studying what appeared to be the dinette table's collapsible center leg.

"I left you some warm water." Nick tucked the loose ends of the towel in the folds around his waist.

"What the!" Sandra bolted upright, spinning around, her hands fisted. She drew one fist back.

Nick held both hands up. "Sorry. Didn't mean to catch you off guard."

"Still in vigilance mode. You're excused." Sandra unfisted her hands. "I suggest you check your towel."

Nick looked down. Two of the folds were undone. The third slipped lower every time he moved. "Hang on."

"I think you need to hang on to your towel." Sandra grinned. "Unless you're into flashing. The only place to streak to is the bathroom."

Nick grabbed the towel with one hand and leaned down, reaching for his duffel. "Thought we might play strip poker in reverse. You know start out buck ass naked and the winner is dressed."

Sandra snorted. She pressed her lips together, trying to inhale deeply. One breath in. A breath out. Another—peals of laughter erupted. "Ok-okay," she managed a few moments later. "I'll take a rain check on the poker match. Let me past you. I'll shower while you figure out the latch on the table leg. You brought sleep shorts, right?"

"Come on, you expect me to sleep clothed?" Nick gripped the towel tighter, inching closer to his duffel.

"Yes. If you're real good, I might. . ." Sandra didn't say more.

"You might what?" Nick straightened, holding the towel in place with one hand and his duffel in his other.

"Never mind." Sandra flung her sleep shirt over her shoulder as she inched closer to the bathroom. "My turn to shower."

"Not until I put my sleep shorts on." Nick backed up into the bathroom and hastily clicked the door shut. As he pulled on his shorts, two thoughts came to mind. He shook his head as he picked up his towel. Sandra had got him good. Left him to his own devices about what she might do. One of them wasn't sleeping nude with him tonight.

NINE

Sandra laid the sheets and blankets on the dinette bench. Did Nick's quick retreat signal something? She'd never known him to be prudish about nudity. He'd used the word naked like it was naughty. Sandra reached for the pillows. Had she miss read the unsaid message? If a naked Nick with a hardon popped out of the bathroom. . .the click of the bathroom door interrupted her train of thought.

"Nick," Sandra said, picking up her sleep shirt. "Are you trying to tell me something?"

Nick tossed his towel over the bathroom door. "What makes you think that?"

"You said naked. Darted into the bathroom like you're hiding. You talked about using condoms earlier with no problem." Sandra moved past Nick.

Nick shrugged. "Yeah, I did. I'm not sure how to bring something up."

"Bring up what?" Sandra hung her sleep shirt on the bathroom doorknob.

"Sex. Sleeping together. It's been three years." Nick turned away. "Never mind. I'll get the table down while you shower."

Sandra put her hand on Nick's arm. He turned partway back to her. "I'm not saying yes tonight. Nor am I saying no to sex overall. We're getting reacquainted in some ways. I remember what fun passion and intimacy with you is."

"You might want to repeat that?" Nick flashed her a grin and winked.

"The fun and passion part, oh yeah! Not when I am sleepy. My mind is already snoring and we're both in the mood. Make sense?" Sandra pulled her t-shirt partway up. "Now you wrestle with the table while I wrestle with the shower."

Nick turned around, saying, "Don't forget your towel."

"I won't."

The rustle of clothes and the click of the bathroom door signaled he could turn around. His wet towel lay on the floor. Sandra's bra, underwear, t-shirt and jeans weren't far from it. A towel hung on the hook half up the outside of the bathroom door. How had he missed the hook? As he picked up his towel, he glanced toward the heater. Two more hooks on the opposite wall came into view. Either his eyesight was failing or he was very tired. The heater's thermostat showed the camper's temperature was in the sixties. Cool yet warm. They might need the double sleeping bag before morning.

Nick rubbed his hands together as he turned. The dinette table's collapsible leg was next. Quick, simple and easy. Unlatch the leg, fold into its storage area underneath the table and . . .

"What the—you're supposed to fold. Stop being stubborn." Nick grabbed the table, tugged and—nothing. "The leg is down. This thing is heavy. Why aren't you moving?"

"Did you undo the back latches?"

Nick started to turn. Sandra came into view. Her towel draped over her shoulder. Her sleepshirt clung in places. Damn, he didn't need unnecessary distractions.

"I'd keep hold of the table unless you want black and blue marks where you least expect it." Sandra hung her towel on the hook next to his.

"Black and blue? Back latches?" Nick gripped the table tighter.

"Yeah, the latches that anchor the table to the wall between the benches. I showed them to you. Didn't I?" Sandra reached for the blanket and sheets she laid on the bench.

"No, you didn't." Nick scowled at her. His lips pressed tightly together. "Take the cushions off and undo the latch on this side."

Sandra stacked the bench cushions near the bathroom door and undid the latch closest to her. She glanced at Nick.

"Can you get around me to do the other side?" Nick rolled his shoulders.

"I think so." Sandra grasped Nick's waist as she moved closer. "Can you move forward?"

"No. I'm not wrestling this table. You're gonna have to snuggle by me as best you can."

Sandra inched behind Nick, sliding her other hand along his waist. A few inches in, flesh slid over flesh. Warmth grazed her palm. Muscle rapidly rippled up, greeting her, massaging her palm and dashing away like a game of tag.

She inhaled and moved behind Nick more. Warm playful hugs from behind images from their past flashed through her mind. Pressing her nude body against his. Reaching around him and gliding her hand lower until she. . .

"Hate to burst our pleasure bubble. This table isn't getting any lighter." Nick shifted the table in his hands as he moved sideways.

Sandra caught her top lip between her teeth. Nick's abs reached up, tapped her palm and rubbed their way across them before they slinked away leaving a scalding trail. Her mind might be tired, but her hormones and psyche were signaling differently. If her nipples got any tauter, she'd have nightshirt peaks to explain. "I'm almost by you. Give me a couple more seconds."

She placed her hand on Nick's hip closer to where she needed to be. Her other she put in the small of his back. Two short breaths and five side steps—"Ok. I'm by you."

"Good. Once you release the one on this side, I'll lower the table."

"I'll help you lower the table." Sandra laid the second set of bench cushions aside, grasped the latch and clicked it open.

"Steady it as I lower it." Nick slowly lowered his arms, working the table between his hand.

Sandra grasped the side closest to her. "It's almost in place."

A thud sounded as the table slid into place.

Nick straightened, yawning. "Let's get this made up. I'm ready to crash."

Ten minutes passed as they placed the cushions and smoothed out the sheets. Sandra tossed her pillow on the bed. "We may need the blanket and the sleeping bag before morning."

Nick tossed his pillow next to hers. "Do we have to bundle?"

Sandra grinned as she unfolded the blanket. "Nah. There's enough room for you and me. Where would we put the bundle?"

"Unfolded like we've got it on top of the sheets covering us."

Nick held up the sleeping bag. "The bunk has more room than this does."

Sandra laughed. "Yeah. Good thing we're sleeping inside."

Nick chuckled. "For sure. You ready to call sides?"

Sandra yawned and sat on the bed. "Sure. Tonight I'll take the inside."

"Works for me." Nick dimmed the lights until a soft nightlight glow filled the camper. He sat next to Sandra. He slipped his arm around her waist and hugged her to him. "Thanks for coming on this adventure with me."

Sandra leaned into the hug, looping her arm around his shoulders. "Thanks for inviting me. I hope my family reunion is less stressful."

Nick snorted. "I'm not laying odds on that. Paparazzi are sneaky."

"We ditched them for now." Sandra stood, yawning. "Time to sleep."

Nick rose, turned back the sleeping bag, sheet and blanket. "Go ahead and get in. I'm putting on a t-shirt. Might need it before morning."

Sandra nodded and scooted over until her feet touched the wall. She pulled the covers over her, unsure she could keep her eyes open much longer.

Nick pulled a t-shirt out of his duffel and put it on. One thing had become evident today, he and Sandra partnered well, united and got things done. How had he missed this before? Had either of them changed? The moments melted away as they worked together. Even the simple dinner and getting the camper set up happened without much preamble or discussion. He inhaled slowly as he turned back toward the bed. Sandra lay on her side facing him, one hand resting on the pillow his head would lay on. Today had shown him something he'd missed before. The thing his heart and psyche kept telling him if he'd just listen. Sandra was the one. Could he believe in the L word his psyche and heart kept whispering? Would Sandra?

Nick glanced around the camper again, noting the door was locked. He pulled the covers over him nestling closer to Sandra as he did. Her breath touched his neck once, twice as he closed his eyes. Right here, right now, in this time and space he felt at peace and at home with probably the one person his heart hadn't forgotten. How long had he been silently in love without realizing it?

Early Thursday Morning

Nick slowly inhaled, squinted one eye open, and quickly closed it. Morning already? As he exhaled, he noticed his breath fogged. Crap, had the heater turned off during the night? He remembered checking on the heater once after going to the bathroom. The outside thermometer showed thirty-two degrees. The heater's thermostat showed sixty-two degrees. Chilly, not uncomfortable.

Sandra had traded places with him after she came back from her bathroom trip. They'd spoon-snuggled, tucking the covers over them as they drifted back to sleep.

"I don't want to get out from under these covers. That air is cold." Sandra snuggled closer to him.

"*Keep your cold feet and hands to yourself.*" Nick jerked as Sandra slid her hand off him. "Move your feet too."

"Come on, one of us has to get warm." Sandra kissed his cheek.

"You're volunteering to get up and check the heater?" Nick tugged the blanket tighter around him.

"You meanie. You'd make me get out into that cold air and. . ." Sandra sniffled.

"Not buying the poor you either. Since I am on the outside, I'll check. I'm wrapping up in the blanket to do it." Nick tugged on the blanket.

"Wait. You can't take the sleeping bag too. Not fair." Sandra grabbed the sleeping bag pulling it back over her.

Tug and pull. Back and forth until Nick rolled over very close to Sandra. "We could get warm another way." He kissed Sandra's cheek, suckled her earlobe between his lips, worrying it with his teeth, and released it. He whispered, his breath hotly caressing her ear. "There's more where that came from. Problem is condoms are in my duffel bag."

"You don't play nice, Nick. Guess I'll have to get up and check the heater." Sandra fanned the covers as she started to toss them off both of them. "Move. I am not crawling over you."

"Dang, you really know how to burst a good. . ." Nick winked at her as he sat up.

Sandra scooted to the edge of the bunk. "Bubble bursting ain't bad, dude. Don't want to bruise precious equipment." She shoved her hand partway up the leg of Nick's shorts and dragged her cold palm down his leg close to his groin.

"No, just chill it into submission." Nick rolled back onto the bunk flinging the covers partially over him. "Guess we'll warm each other up when you and the condoms get back."

"If I come back with the condoms. I'm not going through the duffel to find them." Sandra chafed her arms and hurried toward the rear of the camper. "I'm ready to put socks and thermal underwear on."

Sandra grabbed a towel and draped part of it in front of her. She stepped onto it. She scuffed forward, crossing the floor until she could see the heater's thermostat and the outside thermometer. The outside temperature was twenty-nine degrees. Frost covered part of the window. The heater's temperature was fifty-six degrees. She held out a hand toward the front of the heater. Cold air mixed with intermittent blasts of heat came out of the heater's vent. She tossed the towel over the bathroom door as she darted past it.

"It's freezing outside. The heater is blowing cold air with blasts of heat. We need to call Victor." Sandra scrambled onto the bunk pulling the covers over her.

Nick stuffed his pillow behind his head. "Can't no cell reception. He said I might need an envelope he put in my duffel."

"Where in your duffel? What's in the envelope?" Sandra cuddled closer to Nick.

"I didn't get a chance to ask before we left. Let me get my duffel and find it." Nick pushed the covers off him. "Damn, I swear it's gotten colder in here."

Sandra nodded. "Probably cuz you're uncovered."

Nick scooted to the edge of the bunk and stood. "Keep them covers warm. I might need defrosting when I get back." He leaned down and brushed his lips over hers.

Sandra moved into the warm spot Nick's body heat created while she was gone. She pulled the covers tighter to her, snuggling down into them. Maybe she could create a warm spot for both of them by the time Nick returned.

TEN

"Found it and the condoms too." Nick tossed the box on the bed along with his sweatshirt and a pair of socks. "Want your backpack?"

"Please. Good thing we packed thinking we'd be on the motorcycle." Sandra sat up, wrapping part of the sleeping bag around her.

"Here's your backpack." Nick sat on the bed and pulled his sweatshirt and socks on. "I'm going to see if the microwave works. Hot water for tea and warm sweet rolls sounds good."

Sandra put on her hoodie sweatshirt and a pair of socks. "Sure does. I'll see what's in the envelope."

She took four sheets of folded paper out of the envelope. The first read for Nick. The second read heater instructions. Sandra unfolded the paper and read it aloud.

"Found one with heater instructions on it. Make sure the vents are halfway closed to limit cold air entering the heating coils."

"What else?" Nick put two mugs of water in the microwave and pushed start. The microwave light came on as the carousel began turning. "We got power."

"Good. We need to set the heater's thermostat to seventy to keep the coils and the blower at a steady temperature. Victor's last note is the heater will turn off and on as the inside temperature fluctuates." Sandra picked up the sheet with Nick's name on it. "This one has your name on it."

"Thanks." Nick reached for the envelope. "It's a permission slip from Victor stating we can use the camper. We made sure current registration and insurance papers are in the glove box."

"Thank goodness for Victor thinking ahead. One thing less we have to worry about." Sandra handed him the envelope plus the other folded sheets.

"For sure. I'm going to check on the heater." Nick put all the papers in the envelope as the microwave timer rang.

"I'll take care of the tea. Victor stashed the last of the cinnamon rolls in the fridge as we packed the food."

"Great, we can snack and discuss what comes next." Nick grinned as he scuffed his feet across the floor. "No static sparks to worry about. Warms up my feet fine."

Sandra laughed. "Yes. Socks stay on even under covers for a bit."

"Good thing we took a rain check on my strip poker idea." Nick scuffed his way back to the bed. "Closing the vents helped cut the cold air blasting in. The heat started picking up as I set the thermostat."

Sandra held out a mug of tea. "With sweet rolls, tea doesn't need sweetener."

Nick took the mug and sat on the bed. "Yes. Are you warming the sweet rolls?"

Sandra arched an eyebrow as she sipped her tea. "Depends on if you're asking or demanding."

Nick shook his head. "I know better than to demand." He started to rise as the microwave timer buzzed.

Sandra placed the plate with two rolls plus napkins on the bed. "I have a question."

"Okay." Nick bit into his sweet roll savoring the tart cinnamon and sugar darting across his taste buds as he chewed.

Sandra held up the condom box. "Are you thinking about using these?"

"You got a reason not to?" Nick wiped his mouth and drank more of his tea.

"At the moment, yes. Too damn cold. Other questions needing answers." Sandra picked up her tea mug as she continued speaking. "Do you expect sex, or are you hoping?"

Nick sputtered, tea spewing out of his mouth as he grabbed his napkin. "A loaded question."

"An honest one." Sandra saluted him with her mug.

"Honest and loaded." Nick put his mug and the plate in the sink. "Given our chemistry, expectations ignite. Hoping is the larger item."

Sandra nodded as she put her mug in the sink. "I'm getting back under the covers. Put this..." She held up the condom box. "Where you can easily find it."

Nick held out his hand. "How about where we can both find it?"

"Where would that be?" Sandra tossed the condom box at him. She scooted across the bunk until she was tight to the covers.

Nick caught the box with one hand as he stretched out on the bunk. He placed the box on top of the spot where their pillows overlapped. "Between the pillows. Easy reach for either of us."

Sandra tossed part of the covers over her. Curled up to Nick last night had ignited memories. Memories she hadn't pondered since they'd split up. Nick fueled her desire in ways no other man had. Multiple orgasms, slow passionate kisses, and caresses that had her squirming. His moans as he orgasmed as she suckled him turned her on. Knowing they knew where to touch each other, how to prolong their pleasure and bring their second orgasms to a volcanic pitch—Sandra pressed her legs together. Her nipples stiffened, possibly as stiffened as her clit. "Nice and warm under the covers."

Nick rolled on his side, facing her. "Inviting me in?"

Sandra pressed her lips together. Heat leaped across the small space separating them. Swamping her in its crescendoing wave. Her earlier excuse of cold fled. She'd dreamt of being with Nick like this. Built details into her fantasies and wore out several of her toys. Even ones he had gifted her. Here there were no toys. It was them. Her and Nick. Tasting their chemistry. Knowing that they were able to act upon it. Was Nick ready to go there?

Sandra reached up, cupping Nick's face between her hands. "Yes, come in. Get close and warm us up."

Nick moved closer to her, covering him as he did. "Let's warm each other up."

Their breaths mingled. Sandra gripped Nick's hand. "There's one sure way to do that. Kiss me."

Nick closed the space between them until his forehead rested on Sandra's. Her hair brushed against his fingers as she snuggled closer. Three years since he held her like this. Three lonely years that he hadn't thought about until Garrett suggested asking her to be his date for Paulina and Jackson's wedding. Now the loneliness dissipated. Every breath he took, he got harder. Want pulsed, pushing its way upward, nudging him, reaching toward his heart. Sandra's gaze met his and didn't falter. Without words she signaled she wanted him.

He angled his head slightly, tangled his fingers in Sandra's hair and pressed his lips lightly against hers. Nick slowly parted his lips. Sandra slipped her hand along his waist until her palm warmed the small of his back. Their gazes met as Sandra opened her lips.

Passion and desire mixed with need. Sandra pressed tighter to him with each breath she took. Lowering his hand until it rested on her shoulder refocused his thoughts. He pulled back, breaking off the kiss.

"Are you sure you want to move forward?" Nick rubbed his knuckles along Sandra's jaw. "Mutual consent is a must. I respect you and want you to know your no means no."

Sandra nodded as she spoke. "I understand. Being seen as a person and partner is a turning point for me. I want you to know your no means no, no matter what. Are you ready to move forward?"

Nick entwined his fingers with hers. "Ready when you are."

Sandra snuggled closer until with every breath she took, part of her touched him. Flesh to flesh, yet apart. Nick looped his arm around her waist, cuddling closer.

Nick puckered his lips as he tilted his head. Desire pulsed through him. Bubbling up in places he hadn't expected. His heart skipped a beat each time Sandra's breast brushed against him. Her taut nipples said how much he turned her on. Previously their sex was a heady rush to orgasm and basking in the afterglow. Maybe a second orgasm if the first didn't bliss them out.

Their gazes met briefly as their eyes closed. Their lips met. Firmer against each other this time. Tighter to each other they pressed until heat wrapped them in its coil, enveloping them in their own passionate bubble.

Nick parted his lips, the tip of his tongue venturing forth. Sandra cradled his head, her lips parting as well. He traced the swell of her bottom lip with the tip of his tongue. Traces of cinnamon glided across his tongue as their tongues met. Wave after wave of need and yearning crashed over him, penetrating deep into his core, igniting a fierce splash that flooded downward until he didn't think he could get any harder.

Sandra slowly dragged her fingers down Nick's chest. Every breath he took, every pleasurable shiver rippled over and through her fingertips, sending multi-layered signals to each of her sensual areas. Nick's hand slid up her until he cupped the underside of her breast. His thumb traced over and around her nipple and areola twice. Could she take much more?

Nick's hand slowly moved in up and down caresses. Each coming closer to her mons. His other rest on her hip short of her ass, shoving her hoodie higher until it and her sleepshirt bunched up close to the top of her breasts.

Clothing rubbing over her sensitive peaked nipples set off ripples cascading down and into her. Much more foreplay and she'd. . ."OMG!" Sandra gripped Nick's arm. One burst, followed by another, pulsed straight through her core. She'd forgotten how intense nipple orgasms were. She jerked as Nick caught the nipple closest to him between his teeth, wetting it and her sleepshirt as he flicked his tongue rapidly over and around the extra sensitive tip. Her other nipple throbbed as he squeezed with his thumb and forefinger. Alternating between nipping one nipple, then a squeeze mixed with a slight pull.

Nick whispered hotly against her ear. "And we aren't even undressed. Act two is going to be well worth act one's foreplay."

Nick sat up, pulled his sweatshirt and t-shirt off, tossing both on the foot of the bunk. "I think we need to even things out. You need to take something off now." He fingered the hem of Sandra's sleepshirt. "How about this?"

"Only if we stay under the covers. It's still too chilly to risk getting naked otherwise." Sandra gathered part of her sleepshirt in her hand and tugged. "You willing to shuck clothes that quickly after we put them on?"

Nick smiled and let go of Sandra's sleepshirt. "Not that quickly. We could each take a sock off. Then another piece until we were equally nude."

"Oh, you are trying to seduce me with your intent. You said nude, not naked." Sandra grinned and flipped the covers back over them.

"Much easier to slide hands and lips places than dealing with a mouth full of clothes." Nick rolled on his side. He reached down under the covers and pulled off one sock. He waved it back and forth like a hard-won contested trophy. He tossed the sock over his shoulder. His other followed. "I'm up two pieces. What about you?"

Sandra curled up, wiggled back and forth under the covers and slowly withdrew both hands. "I raise you two socks and call your bluff. You ready to risk baring your cock and balls? Chill em?"

"There's always warm kisses and loving licks to revive them." Nick rolled on his back, arched his hips and shucked his sleep shorts. "Damn that air is cold!"

Sandra pulled her hoodie over her head and tossed it on the foot of the bunk. "Looks like I'm the winner of this strip poker session. I'm still dressed."

Nick rolled toward her, trailed one hand down between her breasts, not stopping until he bunched the hem of her sleep shirt in his hand. "Okay winner, you ready to choose a position for act two?

"*Very* sure." Sandra drew out very as her hand slid down Nick's waist until the tips of her fingers brushed the head of his cock.

Nick jerked, smearing jisim across her palm. "I'd rather be inside you when I come. Sharing a mutual orgasm if possible."

"The most delicious kind of orgasm." Sandra tugged her sleep shirt out of Nick's hand, pulled her sleepshirt over her head and tossed it on the foot of the bunk. "Spoon position. You know the one where your hands and fingers accentuate all my erogenous zones."

Nick swallowed twice. He remembered those places very well. Could he get a condom on without tearing it?

ELEVEN

Nick pulled a condom packet out of the box and held it out. "Gonna need your help getting this on."

Sandra pushed the box of condoms out of the way, took the packet from Nick and opened it. "Covers off. I'll put it on as quick as I can without tearing it."

Nick tossed off the covers and lay back. Sandra grasped him close to his balls with one hand, her other worked the condom down and over him. He pulled up the covers. "I'm very glad we aren't in a tent."

Sandra leaned down and kissed his cock. She drew back smiling. "I agree. Let's get warm."

She rolled on her side and scooted back until her ass and his cock nudged each other. Sandra lifted one leg as she reached between her legs for him. Nick thrust forward, placing him in Sandra's palm. Back and forth they rocked in counter-movement to each other until he slowly slid into warm wetness. Sandra stopped moving.

"Oh, yes. I'm getting warm." Sandra rocked her hips back and forth, working him in and out of her.

Nick wet his thumb and forefinger, captured Sandra's nipple between them and began tugging and tweaking it. He reached between them, coating the fingers of his other hand with her wetness. On her next rock forward, he stroked her clit. Sandra moaned, jerking tighter to him on her backward rock. With each stroke, tug, twist and thrust, the fires of desire burned brighter and hotter. Their rhythm picked up. Sandra shuddered twice, lay still and tightened around him. "I'm almost—there. Yes. There."

Sandra's moans and shivers ignited his orgasm. His eyes closed. Bright bursts of yellows, gold and white exploded across his field of vision.

Several moments of quiet passed. Sandra slowly inhaled as she opened her eyes. Nick lay on his back. His arm covering his eyes. She laid her hand on his chest. "You okay?"

Nick lowered his arm and turned toward her, grinning. "Oh yeah. You?'

"I think so." Sandra pulled the covers up around her shoulders.

"Wanna try for twice?" Nick brushed his lips over hers.

"Not at the moment." Sandra brushed her hair off her face.

Nick chuckled. "Not like we gotta use up all the condoms at once."

"You keeping count?" Sandra picked up the box. "If so, I am doling them out."

"No need. Once we get to Mom and Gram's, I suspect we'll have less chance to use many." Nick tossed the covers off.

Sandra dropped the box on his chest. "I'll worry about that then. Now is time to relax and rest."

"I agree. Be right back." Nick quickly made his way to the bathroom. Kids were a blessing. Something he wanted when he and Sandra were both ready. Not a surprise. He carefully removed the condom, checking for tears or leaks. Close to the top, there was a tear. "Shit, how bad did it tear?"

His hands slicked more as he took the condom off. There was no way to tell how much had leaked out. He washed his hands and groin, tossing the towel over the door as he exited.

Sandra lay on her side, watching him. She patted the space close to her. "It's warmer. Warmer still snuggled up."

"Yeah. Snuggling a bit longer is a good idea." Nick bunched his pillow behind his head and pulled the covers partway over him. "I don't want to alarm you. The condom had a tear at the top. I may have leaked out."

Sandra sat up, tucking the covers under her arms. She let go a deep sigh. "I'm on the pill. My period isn't due for another three weeks. I'm not angry. We'll have to wait and see what happens."

"Do we stop being intimate?" Nick faced Sandra.

"No, if I am pregnant, there's no reason to stop being intimate. We continue to use condoms and be cautious." Sandra laid back. "Are you okay with that?"

"Yes. I want you to know if you are pregnant, I'm prepared to do the right thing."

Sandra laid her fingers on his lips. "Marriage isn't necessary. I'm not trapping you that way. We'll raise our child together. Co-parenting because we're caring and want the best for our child."

Nick cupped Sandra's face. "You're awesome. Remember that."

Sandra licked her lips. Nick pressed his together. Their coupling had all the makings of a quickie. Fast, hot and orgasm driven. The long slow build-up, hands stroking and caressing, heated passion cascading over him and down into. . .Nick jerked.

"You flush nicely. I'd forgotten how good you feel in my hand." Sandra stroked lower on his stomach. If she stroked much lower—he jerked again.

"Are you sure you're ready for round two?"

Sandra turned on her side, facing him. "Glancing up and down is kinda dizzying."

"Focusing is easier when you're on the same level." Nick pulled the covers over them, yawning as he did.

Sandra yawned. "Round two maybe later. I need more sleep." She snuggled closer to him.

"I agree." Nick fluffed his pillow, pulled the covers over his shoulder and exhaled slowly. Sandra blew him a kiss as she closed her eyes. Her warm breath fluttered across his face. Was he faking the feelings his mind and heart kept repeating? She's the one.

Three Hours Later

Nick stretched his arm out. *THWACK!* "Damn, that smarts."

"What happened?" Sandra turned toward him.

"Hit the wall with my hand." Nick flexed his fingers. "I moved over when you went to the bathroom."

"Right in the middle of the bunk. I had to shake you twice before you moved." Sandra raised his hand to her lips, kissing each knuckle. "Sorry."

"Not your fault. I slept deeper than I realized." Nick brushed his knuckles along her cheek.

"I checked the thermostat when I was up. It's sixty-nine degrees inside. Outside is almost forty. Window frost is gone." Sandra sat up and stretched.

"Warm enough to soap and rinse. You wanna go first or me?" Nick rolled on his side.

"I'll go first. Won't take me long. Victor was right about focusing on the simple things for a few days." Sandra scooted to the edge of the bunk and stood. "Simple enough to stay warm and fed."

"To hear my Gram say it, we're living the mortal way. No magic. No spells. No incantations. Roughing it lots." Nick shook his head.

"For this mortal, I'm doing fine. You might be the one roughing it." Sandra stood and turned. "My family camped a lot. Don't know about yours."

Nick nodded as he sat on the edge of the bunk. "Since I got no magic, no shifter traits, and not a late bloomer, I'm as mortal as you."

"Decide what you want for breakfast while I clean up and dress." Sandra started toward the bathroom, stopped, and turned back. "We need to talk about how we're going to handle your mom and gram. Also, your relatives at the wedding."

Nick held up one hand. "The ones attending won't give a damn whether I'm magical or supernatural. Paulina and Jackson have limited magic traits. Mom will fuss some. Gram will echo her a bit."

"And we do lots of PDAs and avoid questions like when are you pregnant and what if your child is magical." Sandra closed the space between her and Nick. She brushed her lips over his and stepped back. "I'm not worried about kids. We got lots of condoms."

Nick pressed his lips together. Score Sandra two, his family. . .well, they had better watch out. Sandra could hold her own.

"Be back in a few." Sandra braided her hair as she decided what clothes she'd wear. She lay a long sleeve top, jeans and clean underwear on her backpack. A fast wet soap and rinse wouldn't take long. If the bathroom were bigger, she'd save water and shower with Nick. No sense pressing their luck. Getting them in the bathroom, door closed and water turned on without causing a flood. . .well, that was not something either of them or Victor needed to deal with.

Two thoughts came to mind as she soaped. They'd done quickies before. There was nothing quick about this morning. It was like a need and desire swamped them, tossed them up on a wave of intense, focused passion and chemistry that washed over them in a huge tidal wave while forcing them into a high plane of pleasure as their orgasms hit. Was this chemistry or more? Her heart thumped harder at the word more. Deity on high, had she fallen in love with Nick again?

Sandra gripped the soap harder. Thoughts of why she couldn't be dashed through her mind. Denial quickly rose to the heap's top and—"I'm letting fear drive. Rear its ugly head and overwhelm me."

She placed the soap in the holder, rinsed and shut the water off. She glanced at the closed door. On the other side were knowns. Items that she could touch, feel and see. Inside her were the unknowns. Feelings she could try suppressing. Let them swamp her, dragging her deeper into their abyss of chaotic panic about what-ifs. She'd learned what ifs could paralyze her if she chose to let it.

Sandra grabbed her towel and started drying off. Each swipe brought her closer to the only choice she had. Dry off, get dressed and face her feeling head-on. She wrapped the towel around her and opened the door. Chilled air slid across her attempting to grip her in its cold tendrils. She spoke as she stepped out of the bathroom. "Left you some warm water. Have you decided what you want for breakfast?"

She gripped the towel tighter with one hand expecting Nick to—"You're naked!"

Nick walked toward her wearing nothing but a grin. "You just noticing that?"

"Uhm...no. You said it wasn't warm enough to streak to the bathroom earlier." Sandra grabbed her clothes, holding them and the towel against her with one hand.

"It's not getting any warmer in here either. I'm dashing to the warm water. You can get an eye full or look away. Nothing new to see." Nick slid past her, pausing long enough to brush his lips over hers.

Sandra didn't move. Swore she didn't blink or breathe until Nick closed the bathroom door. Had she flashed him getting her clothes? Had he gotten—He had gotten a full view from the moment she'd tossed the covers off. Stood up and made her way to the bathroom. Even while she laid out her clothes. She had forgotten how delicious Nick looked nude. Deity help her, if he hadn't mentioned how chilly it was, she'd put her hands in places that would have had them back in the bunk and under the covers using more of the condoms.

She glanced at the bathroom door. Was Nick singing? He wasn't yelping about cold water. She'd heard him sing a few times. Either way, she didn't need to know. If she hesitated dressing much longer, her goosebumps were going to have goosebumps. She tossed her clothes on the bunk, dropped her towel and quickly dressed. As she picked up her towel off the floor, the bathroom door opened. She hoped Nick was able to dry off and dress quick. Another flash of him nude might have her shucking her clothes instead of thinking about fixing breakfast. She spun around, clutching her towel with both hands. Her back to the bathroom.

"Something wrong?" Nick asked.

Sandra inhaled slowly. Two steps forward hung up the towel. One step back and turning around. . .No, she was not ogling Nick. Eye candy was good. Right now too close eye candy and—she swallowed, rubbed her lips together and exhaled. "No. Figuring out what to fix for breakfast."

Nick's breath fanned across the nape of her neck as he slid his arms around her waist, hugging her tight to him. If she leaned back into the hug much more, breakfast might turn into brunch.

Nick suckled Sandra's earlobe between his lips, worrying it with his teeth. He let go and whispered in her ear. "Appetizer for later."

He hugged her tight to him and let go. He didn't need to look down to know how the hug affected him. Keeping his zealous id and male hormones under control might call for another shower. A cold one. Nick tossed his towel over the bathroom door. He focused on one word. Clothes. The sooner he got them on, the sooner his psyche might refocus.

TWELVE

"I've got an idea for a tune if we do the festival. Just me and my guitar. Without a band, I'm sure no one would recognize me." Nick pulled on his briefs and jeans.

"Let's eat and talk about it. I need coffee. I think Victor put some in one of the boxes. He said his cone drip brewer was in the cabinet next to the dining area." Sandra sat on the bunk putting on her socks and hikers.

"Must be what I heard rattle when I hit my hand on the wall." Nick pulled on his t-shirt and sweatshirt. He sat next to Sandra, putting his socks and hikers on. "Gonna need to put the bunk up to use the table."

"I'll make the coffee while you wrestle the bunk." Sandra started folding the sleeping bag.

"Tackling and wrestling were last night's thrills. Today's are folding covers." Nick grabbed one end of the sheet Sandra pulled toward her. "Working together gets coffee made sooner."

"For sure. My sister Emily and I referred to folding laundry as wrestling matches when it came to towels and sheets." Sandra took the folded sheet from Nick. "We can stack blankets, sheets and pillows on one of the benches."

"Means we're sharing a bench for eating." Nick winked and added. "Something to be said for cozy and close."

"Also means spattering, coffee spills who knows where and elbow jabs." Sandra stacked the pillows on top of the covers. "I gave up food fights in the seventh grade."

Nick pulled the two cushions covering the table off the bunk, leaning them against the wall. "Coffee's just not my color. It goes so much better inside than outside and in splotches."

Sandra snickered, pressed her lips tighter together, and looked away. Snorts and more snickers sounded.

Nick unfolded the table leg and lifted the table into place. "Yeah, my comedic timing sucks. Lenny says it's a good thing I can carry a tune as well as I do."

Sandra wrapped her arms around her sides. Laughter rang out. She sat on the bunk, wiping her eyes. "Memory flashed through my mind. That picture of you in that tye-die suit, dressed to the nines and your date in the paisley print formal."

"Ah yes, the picture from my senior year homecoming. Fashion faux pas." Nick sat on the bench opposite Sandra.

"I'm sure you were very happy when you got that photo out of the house."

"Mom swore up and down I let a mortal dress me. I did, me. Tanya and I wore our fave get-ups. Homecoming theme was fave fashion era. I chose the eighties. Tanya chose the seventies. We had a great evening laughing, dancing and hanging out as friends." Nick laid his hands on the table. "You're doing coffee. I am fixing what?"

Sandra combed her fingers through her hair, working it into a loose ponytail. "I think you can handle toast and sausage. Microwave and toaster oven duty. I'll make the eggs."

Nick stood, saluting her. "Reporting for toast and sausage duty ma'am."

"First we find the coffee and the coffee maker. I'll get the water heating while you find the coffee." Sandra turned the burner on under the pan she'd filled with water.

Nick nuzzled her neck as he slipped past her. PDA practice had started. If they kept the chemistry this hot, practicing responses wasn't necessary.

"Found it." Nick held up the bag.

"Hazelnut Mocha. I'm glad we got the cinnamon-flavored creamer." Sandra turned the heat down on the burner under the skillet she put two pats of butter in. She cracked four eggs into the skillet and stirred. Next, she added bits of cheese from the slice she tore up.

Nick filled the drip filter with the coffee. "Ready to pour and brew when you are."

Sandra held out the wooden cooking spoon to Nick. "You watch the eggs. They're almost done. Stir them a couple of times."

Nick took the spoon and stepped back. "Do you need help with lifting the pan to the carafe?"

Sandra shook her head. "No, going to set it in the sink and use a mug to get the water into the filter."

Nick picked up the carafe. "I'll get it. I think the eggs are done."

Sandra turned off the burner under the skillet and pan of water.

Nick placed the carafe in the sink next to the pan, steadying it. Sandra poured two mugs of water into the filter brewer. Sounds of coffee dripping into the carafe and the aroma of fresh brewing coffee filled the air.

Nick placed the carafe and brewer back on the table. "What do you think about doing the festival tonight?"

"I don't know. Laying low makes sense. Part of me says mingling and blending in does too. What do you think?" Sandra set two plates of scrambled eggs on the table.

Nick put two slices of toast and a couple of sausage links on each plate. "There's chance one of us might be recognized. At least there's no blasted paparazzi tailing us. We can't hide forever. I'm still thinking about it."

"I agree. We can ask Wanda about the festival later." Sandra placed utensils, napkins and mugs next to the plates. "Do you still drink your coffee black and sweet?"

"Depends on how strong the coffee is." Nick filled one mug and sipped. He added honey and creamer to the mug, stirred and sipped again. "A bit of honey and the cinnamon coffee creamer add up to a perfect first cup."

Sandra filled her mug, added creamer, sipped and closed her eyes. "Nirvana. Hot coffee, warm food, and blessed quiet. Are you sure we have to go back?"

Nick saluted her with his mug, sipped twice and set the mug down. He pulled his plate to him. "At some point, yes. For now, no."

Sandra spread her napkin across her lap, speared a fork full of eggs. "Here's to good company, a great simple meal, and time for two cups of coffee."

Nick nodded. "Yes. Time to eat without looking over your shoulder or rushing."

Moments passed as they ate in companionable silence. Nick got up from the table. "Where did we put the bag with the books and notebooks?"

Sandra wiped her mouth. "Look in the hanging bunk. Victor put some of the last stuff he brought out up there."

"More coffee?" Nick held up the carafe. "I'll refill it after I find a notebook."

"I'll get the coffee." Sandra put their plates in the sink. "You been humming. Song idea?"

Nick nodded. "Yeah, came to me as I slept. Bits and pieces. Words and phrases."

"Care to share?" Sandra filled the filter with fresh coffee grounds and water.

"Can't. My muse works in spurts. I jot down ideas and chords here and there. Once I get a stanza or two, I start figuring out the storyline." Nick laid the pad and pen on the table. "I'll play the melody for you later. You gonna have to wait for the lyrics until the festival."

"You've decided?" Sandra refilled their mugs and placed the two remaining sweet rolls on napkins beside the mugs.

"Kinda. If we do the festival, I'll have the song ready. How about we sing together? What do you think?" Nick sat down, sipped his coffee, and took a bite of his sweet roll.

Sandra set her mug down. "What you got in mind? Been a while since I sang in public. Since our last choral concert at our high school graduation."

"Remember the one I wrote for the fall musical, Together Again?" Nick flipped through the notepad he laid on the table. "The couple realizes people are trying to matchmake them."

"The song about the couple realizing they're fated mates?" Sandra finished her sweet roll.

"That's it. Do you remember the lyrics?' Nick pushed the notepad to her.

"Vaguely. There's a line that goes, here we stand fated to be together." Sandra picked up her mug. "Are you suggesting that we're fated mates?"

Nick snorted. "If that was true, do you think we'd be sitting here reminiscing? We probably be married with kids."

Sandra leaned down, trying to see under the table. Were Nick's fingers crossed?

"Drop something?" Nick leaned down, caught her staring intently at his hand. He flexed it, wiggled his fingers and put his hand on the table.

"No. Wondering if you crossed your fingers." Sandra finished her coffee. "That's enough coffee for now. Do you remember the melody for..." Sandra pulled the notepad to her. "Together Again?"

"Chords are written in the margin. Lenny wanted me to demo this song for my next CD. I rewrote the lyrics and added a chorus. We can do the first two stanzas and the chorus." Nick picked up his guitar and strummed. "You take the first stanza. I'll sing the second. We'll do the chorus together."

Sandra cleared her throat. "Okay. I might be a bit off-key."

"Don't worry. We'll practice. Right now, let's try it out." Nick strummed a chord. "Is that too high?"

"I don't think so." Sandra pulled the notepad closer to her. She wet her lips, inhaled and sang.

"Look at us standing here together.

Who knew what happened?

It was magical.

Me and you belong together.

I knew I'd never go anywhere without you.

Time always stops when I look at you."

Nick kept playing as he sang the second stanza.

"You and me side by side.

Our connection is stronger this time.

Who knew how magical it could be?

What our hearts and minds denied.

Will it work out this time?

Or are we fooling ourselves?"

Nick stopped playing. "Not bad for our first time through."

"I agree." Sandra tapped the page. "Where's the chorus?"

Nick turned a couple of pages. "A few pages back. I decided to rewrite that again. I'm still working on it. Here's what I got so far."

Sandra turned the notebook so both of them could see it. "Go ahead and play while I sing what you got."

Nick played the first three chords. Sandra hummed a bit and nodded. "Got it."

"Okay, on three. One—Two—Three." Nick replayed the chords shown.

Sandra sang:

"Together again,

Do we want to take the step?

Our hearts keep saying yes.

Do we listen when our minds say no?

Are we stronger enough to make it last?

Accepting what our hearts say with every beat,

Together is our fate."

"I like that. It flows and the melody is up-tempo without being too jazzy or rock-oriented." Sandra leaned back.

"Contemporary ballad with a bit of country rock." Nick laid his guitar on top of the stack of pillows and blankets.

"You want to try it together?" Sandra stretched.

Nick stood. "Later. I'm going to check on the water tank. Empty the gray water tank in the sewer drain I saw last night."

"Need some help?" Sandra scooted to the edge of the bench.

"Not really. I think better when I am puttering and alone. How about we go for a short walk once I'm done?" Nick zipped up his jacket and pulled on his gloves and hat.

Sandra shrugged. "Okay. I'll clean up in here."

Nick laid his hand on Sandra's shoulder. "It's not you. I write like this even with my band. I get in my head and hear the music and words. I shut people out. Give me about fifteen minutes, twenty max and I'll be ready to take that walk."

Sandra stood, looped her arms around his neck and pressed her lips to his. Her lips parted as her tongue traced his top lip. Nick slowly slid his hand down Sandra's back, stopping close to her ass. He met her tongue with his, opening his mouth to her, pulling her closer until they pressed tightly against each other. Tastes, sips and caresses inched internal temperatures higher.

Nick pulled back, breaking off the kiss. "Whoosh. I better get those chores done. Got my imagination fueled. Creativity sparked and well—can't use up the condoms in one day."

Sandra fanned herself. "Hopefully, it's warmer outside. Though if I'm as flushed as you are, we're both fueled up for what needs done."

Nick brushed his lips across Sandra's again. "I'm behaving. See you in fifteen minutes."

He didn't look back as he opened the camper door. If he did, both water tanks, grey and fresh, were going to need double emptying and refilling.

Sandra sat down, unsure what had happened. Nick had walked away from her? Told her he wasn't interested in—ah frack who was she fooling? Her insecurities were running rampant for no apparent reason. Were they? The last time they'd sung that song together, they presented it to the senior year play committee.

Fifteen years ago, she'd dreamed about her and Nick being a couple. It hadn't worked out. Three years ago, they tried again with a bit better success. What made now different?

You're finally listening to your heart. Hearing the yes, he's the one. Paying attention to what you're feeling when he touches you. Chemistry ignites many things. Your heart sparked its message.

If she told Nick how she felt, would he. . .there was no predicting what either of them would say. Sandra let go a deep sigh, stretched and stood. "I could spill it all now or wait. Wait for what I am not sure. My heart races when I think about telling Nick how I feel. Then I wonder do I trust me? Am I secure enough to continue to pull this off if he says he's not interested in more?"

She shook her head, glanced around the camper, and let go another sigh. They were in this for the time being. Opportunities to talk and get closer were gifts. Gifts that they hadn't had previously. Taking advantage of those gifts was important.

Chores were one thing that could keep her mind off speculations. Insecurity didn't like to shut up. It brayed loud and clear whenever it got out. Corralling it and gagging it happened now. Sandra washed and dried each dish. She focused on each task she could do. Putting dishes away, wiping down the table—checking on where her heart and head were. Sandra glanced out the rear window as she checked whether the towels were dry and the heater's temperature. Nick leaned against the van. His lips moving. She couldn't make out any of the words he said. Wait, was he singing?

THIRTEEN

Nick hummed and tapped his fingers on his leg. The second verse needed work. The chorus really needed. . .acceptance. His heart was in those words. The words he'd avoided for some time. He needed a mate. He needed to stop avoiding the obvious. He found her. Now to stop faking his feelings. Speak what his heart kept telling him. He slowly inhaled and let go a deep sigh. He hummed a short melody.

"There's only one answer.
My heart knows what I haven't said.
I'm in love.
How could I miss what was right before me?
It's you, only you.
Others came and went.
You moved in and stayed.
No other ignites my heart like you."

His thoughts flittered back to the image he painted as he sang the chorus for what he tentatively titled Believe in Love. He believed in love's elusive tempting call. The illusion it painted for him time after time before—*Stop fooling yourself. You know Sandra's the one. Attempting to rationalize what you feel isn't completely possible. Logic isn't always logical.* Blast his psyche was right.

Dude, timing is important. Place that is up to you and your heart. Listen and know. You'll know when it's the right time and place. Thank Lupa, his conscience didn't bill for therapy. Otherwise, he'd have one hell of a bill.

He inhaled, focusing on the clouds and blue sky. He'd tossed aside the substandard person many of his family tried to stick the label on him. He'd broken free, became the person he envisioned and yet. . .Nick slowly exhaled. He still had bits and pieces of the kid that wanted to belong, fit in and be accepted for himself. That part dwindled and faded the more he was with Sandra. So what if he could do magic like the rest of his family? His mom and gram accepted him for the most part. Maybe total acceptance came when he showed he was comfortable in his own skin. Accepted himself and liked who he was, magical or not. Keyword was believe. Believe in him, believe in what he and Sandra shared, chemistry, closeness, and caring that had and was evolving. Did he spill his heart now? Wait? Was there a perfect time and place?

Nick unfastened the gray water tank hose and put it away. He checked the water tank. It was full. Both clanks and thumps were the pumps shutting off.

As he put away the water tank hose, he smiled. Twenty minutes of work and focus brought him peace. Peace of mind knowing that he had the chorus ready for Believe in Love and peace of mind knowing his heart and psyche were of one accord. He was in love. Had been for a while. He hadn't taken time to listen to his own quiet voice within. He was done with worrying about finding a place to belong. He already had. His music, Sandra, and where they went from here mattered more than appeasing his magic relatives, his prior sense of trying to fit in where he couldn't and wouldn't. Who he was was enough and if someone didn't like it, okay they were entitled to their feelings and opinions. His were the *only* ones that mattered.

Nick latched the storage bin closed. He rubbed his hands together and blew on them. Chill in the air remained. He could smell the leaves and earth changing settling in for their winter rest and rejuvenation. His Uncle Alfred's saying came to mind as the wind blew and stirred the leaves close to his feet. Life forces know who the magical ones are. You don't need hocus pocus and magic spells to be at one with the universe and all of creation's deities.

Magic logic worked differently than mortal logic. Magic logic believed in the impossible. The ability to create and manifest personal magic was possible if he believed in himself and his innate abilities. Magic flowed through everything. Everything lived, breathed, and pulsated its own special magic. Rocks pulsated rock images, qualities and their own life form. Trees as well. Inanimate and animate items projected their cellular being.

Nick agreed. Perhaps his magic was enhanced smelling, his strong intuition and keen understanding, plus his musical ability. Someone tracing the family's ancestry said that a great great aunt thrice removed sang with an angelic voice, almost perfect key and pitch. He shrugged. Bits and pieces of his ancestors' gifts were awesome. They gave part of themselves as they lived, loved and created the next generations. He wondered what Sandra would say when he told her. Would she stay or was he opening himself to rejection?

Sandra leafed through Nick's song notebook. Bits and pieces of lyrics and chords filled quite a few pages. Together Again was the main piece he had ready to use. The next page had words, phrases and a few chords on it. At the top of the page, the words in caps read Believe in Love. Easy to do if they weren't faking things. Frack, she didn't know how much longer she could keep her guarded heart safe.

How did she safely believe in love? Was there any way to love without risking her heart? Risking was part of loving her mother and grandmother admonished the first time she'd come home with a broken heart. How many times did her heart have to break before she—what? Gave up? Turned her back on what could be instead what her subconscious drummed up based on past experience? If she'd given that any credence, she wouldn't be here now. She valued Nick's trustworthiness on many levels. He kept his word and commitments. They'd mutually agreed their prior attempts hadn't worked out. Sandra swiped her palms down her jeans as she stood. Time had come to get out of her protective cocoon and let go of the past. A new beginning was unfolding here and now. A new start that could go anywhere they decided. She hoped they were on the same wavelength and path.

The outside door opened as she refilled the carafe filter with fresh coffee grounds. Nick quickly closed the door behind him, holding out a flyer. "I hope you don't mind. I asked Wanda what time the festival starts."

Sandra shrugged. "Saves me bundling up to do it with you."

Nick grimaced. Crap, had he overstepped again? "I'm sorry. Thought I'd get the info without committing us." He laid the paper on the table. How badly had he messed up?

Sandra poured hot water into the carafe filter. She set two mugs on the table along with a small tin of butter cookies. "There's nothing to be sorry about. I would have gone with you. We both probably have questions. Now we've got some info. What did you tell Wanda?"

Nick hung up his jacket. "I asked her where I could get more info on the festival. She gave me the flyer and said if we had more questions, she'd be happy to answer them."

"Did you say we were interested in attending?" Sandra set the empty pan in the sink.

Nick sat down. "No. I thanked her for the info and said if we were interested in attending, we would let her know."

Sandra took the filter out of the carafe and set the carafe on the table. "The flyer says attendees provide talent. If we do, duet only or is your other song ready?"

Nick filled his mug. "I need to finish the words for my song. Are you saying you want to go?"

Sandra sat down and filled her mug. "Are you sure you want to do this? Take a chance we might be recognized?"

"If we are, no paparazzi are going to find us that quickly. Sylvan Valley is not a large spot on the map." Nick creamed and sweetened his coffee. He stirred it and drank some.

Sandra shrugged. "We're taking a chance regardless of what we do. A few more days peace and quiet would be nice."

"Agreed. The festival gives us cover. With intermittent broadband availability, we aren't going to hit social media quickly either." Nick munched two cookies out of the tin.

Sandra sipped her coffee. She wrapped both hands around the mug, looked away and back at him. She let go of the mug as she spoke. "I've got to get the brownie cakes made. You've got a song to finish. We need a bit of lunch too."

"We're going?"

"Yes, with one stipulation." Sandra ate a cookie.

"All right what is it?" Nick set his empty mug down.

"You finish your song and go first." Sandra closed the cookie tin, finished her coffee, and stood. " If folks like your singing, we'll do the duet."

Nick grinned. He held up his hand, palm toward Sandra. "Better we do the duet first. I can do my solo later on. I'll finish the song while you make the brownie cakes. Remember you need for twenty-five people."

Sandra clapped her palm to his. " All right, duet first. Your solo second. I'm sure Wanda has the few extra ingredients I need to stretch the cake mixes and chocolate bits we've got."

Nick kept his thoughts to himself. Sandra could cook and food wasn't the only thing. His libido and hormones were close to boiling over. He glanced at his watch. Twelve-thirty PM. Day half over. Nothing much done. Yet, there was a lull in the air, a feeling of peace, not broken pieces of small moments of tranquility. He wanted to do the festival, try out his new song, sing with Sandra and enjoy being himself. Not his on-stage persona who sang because he needed to make a buck. At the festival, he could be Nick who enjoyed singing and making music. His passion for telling stories with lyrics and music got him juicy. Juicy in the moment. Revved his hormones and libido until his vibrations orgasmed as his music birthed itself. Could anyone else understand? Perhaps Lenny and Victor were right; his magic was his music-making abilities, his storytelling song lyrics and his bonus was he could carry a tune whether with a band or by himself.

"I'm hungry. How about some lunch?" Nick grinned. "No, my infamous teenage buzzsaw appetite hasn't returned."

Sandra sighed. "I remember the time the varsity football player challenged you to the hot dog eating contest with chili, onions and hot sauce on them."

"Yeah, took us all three lunch periods to do it. Speed wasn't part of the contest. I ate five hot dogs. He couldn't finish his fifth."

"Yes, both of you reeked of onions and hot sauce for the rest of the day." Sandra opened the fridge. "Grilled ham and cheese, okay?"

"Sure. I can make them while you let Wanda know we're attending the festival and check on the extra ingredients you need for the brownie cakes." Nick set the skillet Sandra handed him on the stove. He hoped Wanda didn't ply Sandra with twenty questions trying to get more info on them.

Sandra pulled the camper's door closed. Wind whipped up a few snowflakes around her feet. She put her hands in her jacket pockets and stepped out from the protection of the pool house overhang and the camper. Blasts of wind picked up as she entered the open space between their campsite and the main building. She ducked her head and picked up her pace.

The wind died down the closer she got to the main building. Sandra glanced up. Light and dark browns intermittently peeked out from their snowcapped covers. Patches of green intermixed with brilliant golds and reds dotted part of the mountains slopes. Occasional bursts of orange broke up the pattern. It was as if nature sent a morse code message to the world saying see me, look at the beauty that is around you, be one with the force of life that pulsates through all of us.

Sandra stomped and wiped her feet on the doormat as she pushed the main building's front door open. Warmth skirted across her face and cheeks beckoning her welcome. Sandra took off her hat and unzipped her jacket.

Wanda waved and approached the registration counter. "Hey Sandra. Help you with something?"

"I was wondering if I could use your kitchen and get a few extra ingredients I need for the brownie cakes I'm making for the festival tonight." Sandra picked up the pen next to the registration book and pulled the notepad next to it to her. "I need four eggs, a stick of butter and some vegetable oil. If I can use a couple of pans too, that would be awesome. I'll clean up behind myself."

"Sure, you can use the main kitchen. Ralph, our head cook, can help you with the items and pans you need. Don't worry about cleanup. Ralph can run the pans through the dishwasher with the rest of the dishes from his prep. You ready to start now?"

"Not yet. After lunch, I'll be back with the mixes and what ingredients I have." Sandra handed Wanda the pad. "Here's what I need. If you've got confectioner's sugar, that would be great. Sprinkled on the cake mixed with crushed peppermint candies kicks the sweetness up a few notches."

"I'll check with Ralph on what else he might have." Wanda tore the sheet off the pad. "Glad you and Nick are attending tonight. Most of our guests are going. See you after lunch."

Sandra zipped up her jacket, put her hat on and started toward the door. That was easy. Wanda hadn't asked if they were going to entertain too.

"Sandra, one moment," Wanda called out. "Nick asked about the entertainment earlier. Do you want me to add the two of you to the entertainment list?"

Sandra wet her lips, turned around and said, "Have to talk it over with Nick. We'll let you know. Gotta run. Nick is preparing lunch."

She bolted out the door, almost running. Much more faking without talking it over with Nick might have their story full of holes and inconsistencies. Keeping the story straight for his mom and gram plus her mother and other nosy relatives. . .they had to come up with one right now. She hoped Nick had his song together because they had other things to discuss.

FOURTEEN

Late Thursday Afternoon

Nick strummed the chords he'd written for the chorus of his new song. A slow melodious build-up until he spoke his heart. The lyrics were true. He'd fallen in love without a clue. His heart kept telling him he was in love. He didn't listen. This time he was listening. He heard the words loud and clear. How did he tell Sandra he wanted the real thing? Had the faking gone too far? He hoped not.

Nick laid his guitar aside as Sandra opened the camper door. Her wide-eyed look said more than if she'd spoke as she entered. Nick rose, holding his hand out. "You okay? Sandwiches are done. I'll warm them in a moment. "

"I-I'm okay. Wanda threw me with something she asked me." Sandra slowly exhaled, unzipping her jacket.

"Only one question?" Nick laid his hand on Sandra's shoulder. "Let me help you with your jacket. Catch your breath."

Sandra stuffed her hat in her jacket pocket. She quickly took her jacket off. "I appreciate the offer. Is there any coffee left?"

"I finished the last cup. How about some tea or hot chocolate while I warm the sandwiches?" Nick took the sandwiches out of the skillet, put them on a plate and placed them in the microwave. "It'll take a couple of minutes to warm them."

Sandra tossed her jacket on the bench closest to her. "We've got to talk. Get our story figured out. I'm afraid I'll say something different than what you've said and boom, we're caught."

Nick nodded as he set a mug of tea in front of her. She wrapped both hands around the mug. The warmth seeped deep into her hands. She raised the mug, sipped and set it down. Nick had prepped it like she had hers last night, sweet with a bit of cream. He paid attention; he focused on them and what she did. Her heart skipped a beat as he pressed his lips to her forehead.

"Food first. You can tell me what happened while we eat." Nick set a plate holding a sandwich and chips in front of her. He set a similar plate on the table across from her.

"Thanks for making lunch. I appreciate you chipping in." Sandra bit into her sandwich. Gouda, munster, and the honey ham taste glided across her tongue and taste buds. Each was distinct and mixed together. What was the tangy part? A hint of mustard? Nick had grabbed a few packets when they were at the convenience store.

"Nick, did you add mustard to the sandwiches?" Sandra wiped her mouth, sipped some of her tea and leaned back against the bench's cushioned back.

"Sure did. Just a couple dabs on each sandwich. Give it some zing." Nick tore his sandwich in half and took a bite.

"Good choice. I like. Nice to know you have some culinary talents." Sandra broke a chip in two, eating one half. "I told Wanda I would get back to her on making the brownie cakes after lunch."

"Okay. Fine with me. Gives me time to practice my solo. We can practice our duet after lunch if you like." Nick took a bite of the other half of his sandwich, chewed and swallowed. "What else did you and Wanda talk about?"

"Attending the festival. I confirmed that since we decided to go." She paused, waiting for Nick to confirm.

"We did."

Sandra sipped her tea, set her mug down and continued her thought. "Wanda asked about adding us to the festival entertainment. I told her I had to talk with you about that."

Nick held up his palm to her. "High five on that!"

Sandra laid her palm against Nick's. Warmth brushed her palm and ebbed. She lowered her hand. "Thanks. I didn't want to commit and you decided not to. That spooked me when I thought about how much we haven't talked about yet about our made-up story. Faking it is not easy."

Nick pushed his mug and plate aside. He leaned forward, placing his palms on the table. "What if we stopped faking it?"

"What?" Sandra stared at him wide-eyed, her mouth moving. No other words spoken.

"Hear me out for a moment, please. I want to talk about what is going on here for me." Nick touched the center of his chest and his head.

Sandra wet her lips and nodded. "I'll try." She toyed with her napkin.

Nick leaned back, put his hand back on the table, palm up. "Three years ago, I thought I wanted freedom. Free to come and go. No strings attached and pursue my music."

"I remember you saying you needed to focus on your career. Build a following. I asked how I could help. You said by letting you go."

Nick nodded. "I was a dumb ass."

Sandra rolled her eyes. "Your call."

"Yup. I accept I fucked up real good." Nick cupped his hand around Sandra's. "I realize I wasn't listening to my heart. I had tunnel vision and it was very selfish."

Sandra looked down at their entwined hands. Was he trying to soften the blow? Say he made the same mistake again? She blinked her eyes, trying to hold back the fear, swallow what her gut kept yelling at her. *He's dropping you again.*

She wasn't sure how much more she could take.

Nick scooted to the end of the bench, rose and picked up their dishes. "Do you mind moving over? I want to sit next to you."

Sandra opened her mouth, ready to decline. Her palms and nose itched. The hair on the back of her neck prickled. Her stomach kept flip-flopping with each beat of her heart. A high-pitched ringing started in her right ear. As the ringing faded, one thought flooded her mind. *You need to hear him out. Trust your heart, trust you. Hear him clearly without trying to surmise what he isn't saying.*

She moved over. "Is there more tea?"

"Enough for a half mug each." Nick emptied the carafe into their mugs. He put the carafe in the sink as he continued speaking. "We're good friends. Trust each other. Or we wouldn't be here."

Sandra sipped some tea, set her mug down and turned so she faced Nick as he sat next to her. "I'm trying to hear you out. Part of me keeps tossing up our foul-ups."

Nick laid his hand on hers. "I'm guilty of that too. Right here and now, I'm focusing on us. What you mean to me. How special you are. Things I tried to ignore thinking I wanted something else. I thought if I got a magical partner somehow I'd make up for what I wasn't."

"Wow," Sandra whispered. "When did you change your mind?"

Nick chuckled and shook his head. "About the time Garrett asked me why I wasn't accepting myself. Who was I trying to impress? Mom. Gram and others in my family?"

"Loaded questions for sure." Sandra drank more of her tea.

"My answer blew me away. I couldn't answer. I knew I had to find myself. Be who I wanted to be, accept myself as I am and understand there's parts of me that aren't going to change. Like I am non-magical. Nothing wrong with that. I love making music and writing songs." Nick slipped his arm around her shoulders.

"You're comfortable in your own skin? At peace with who you are?" Sandra tipped her head back, making it easier for her to see Nick's eyes.

"Yes. All that and more." Nick cupped her cheek. "I'm listening to my heart. Hearing my psyche and the message both are and have been shouting for the last three years. I love you. I'm in love with you."

"*You're what*?" Sandra pressed her lips tighter together. He said the words she'd hoped to hear. The three words that she longed to hear three years ago. Wanted to hear now. Why did she doubt him? Could she believe in love? Accept the one person she'd given a large part of her heart to return her feelings?

"Nick, how am I supposed to believe that you love me?" Sandra scooted back as far as she could on the bench.

"It's important that we look each other in the eye and own our feelings. Are you telling me you don't care for me?" Nick took his arm from around her shoulders.

"We're talking about something that wasn't the initial intent. Why hadn't we been this frank before?" Sandra slumped against the wall, almost in the corner.

"Because we didn't take time to see each other, toss away the clutter of expectations and our personal experiences with other tried relationships."

Sandra exhaled slowly. "Here we're away from prying eyes, the damn paparazzi, and your adoring public."

"I *don't* want to be adored, groped, and flattered by anyone else but you. Fans are okay. People who like my music and want to buy my CDs and music downloads plus come to my concerts are awesome." Nick paused, pointing at her. "It's not them I want to come home to every night. It's you. You listen. You challenge me. You get me hot and bothered."

Sandra ducked her head. "Thanks. You turn me on too. We got chemistry for sure."

"I appreciate your approval rating." Nick pressed his lips to hers and pulled back. "If you are pregnant, a little boy or girl conceived out of our passion and caring is awesomeness. If you're not, that's okay too."

"Why did you add that?" Sandra held her hands out. "I need some space. Can you sit on the other side, please?"

"Sure." Nick moved to the opposite side of the table. "I want you to know I'm not saying this because the condom tore."

Sandra faced him, her hands palms down on the table. "Trust is an important part of a relationship. How do I know you're not faking it? Practicing a story you came up with to tell our families."

"Trust is important. I think it's time we trust ourselves, our hearts and each other. We trust each other to a point. Can you tell me what your heart and mind are saying?"

Sandra held up three fingers. "First, I know you are trustworthy or I wouldn't be here. We're friends, probably best friends in a lot of ways, and our shared past gives us a solid foundation that our friendship and mutual trust are built upon."

"Agreed. Go on."

"Second, I don't fuck. Sex is good. My battery-operated boyfriend does a good job on a non-emotional basis. Granted I gotta replace the batteries from time to time."

Nick smiled and winked. "I'm glad I'm beating out the battery dude."

"Third, I love you too. Probably been in love with you since our junior year of high school. You were out of reach. The magic vs. mortal class split was all too real." Sandra turned her hands over, laying them palms up. "Where do we go from here? Deal with any doubt that remains?"

Nick laid his palms on hers. "Doubt and fear are powerful when you don't talk about them. What fears do you have?"

"All of this will disappear once we're back in Cauldron Falls. Here it's just us. There it's our families, your fans, my job, and your career. Stresses we don't have here."

Nick slid his fingers and palm lower until his thumb lay close to her wrist pulse point. "My great aunt told me that heartbeat love magic is one of the strongest magics there is. It's a natural force not even the oldest magic traits can break. If you lay your other hand the same way on my other hand, we can feel each other's heartbeat. Tell me, how you feel and see how my heart responds."

FIFTEEN

Sandra moved her fingers and thumb lower until she could feel Nick's pulse. She closed her eyes, inhaled, counting in the one magic-numbered sequence she remembered from her attempt at learning magic. She moved her thumb closer to Nick's wrist pulse point. One beat, two beats. Steady and strong. She pressed her lips together, envisioning what her heart and psyche pulsed each time she touched Nick. Sandra slowly opened her eyes, looked up until Nick's gaze met hers. "Nick Morgan, I love you. I don't want us to be fake. I don't want our engagement to be fake. I want you as part of my here and now, my future and life partner. I don't want fear and doubt to drive."

With each word she said, Nick's strong heartbeat pulsed against her thumb. His gaze never wavered. A glow reached out to her, drawing her in and embracing her in ways she'd never experienced with any of her other relationships.

Nick brushed his thumb across Sandra's pulse point. He noted how steady and strong her heartbeat was as she declared her feelings and intentions. Great Aunt Chloe told him all living forces were born with love magic. Understanding how it worked befuddled even the sagest magic and wisest mortal from the beginning of recorded history. Some things were beyond understanding. Good thing too because deities and the One set love magic in motion for the betterment of life, not for an elite few to control and dictate.

"Sandra Cunningham, I don't want us to be fake. I don't want our engagement to be fake. I loved you. I love you now and plan to for the rest of our lives together. I want to be part of you're here and now, your life and future partner."

He slipped the engagement ring off her finger, let go of her hand and rose. He faced the table, dropped down on one knee, holding his palm out with the ring on it. "Will you do me the honor of getting engaged again? This time with real intent, no more fake."

Sandra picked up the ring and placed it on her finger. "Real intent, yes. Engaged again, yes. No more faking."

Nick cupped Sandra's face, brushed his lips across hers. "Hate to change topic, but we've got a festival to get ready for."

Sandra snorted. "Note for future. We make time to relax and TLC us. Both of our jobs demand travel, busy focused attention when we're at work."

Nick nodded as he sat down across from Sandra. "Very true. One thing Lenny kept telling me was to take time off, relax, and take care of me. Burnout is a large problem in show business. You can't turn gigs down. Money comes from touring, recording and promoting."

"It does. Maybe we can combine part of that together. Copy editing and copywriting are related. Promo materials are part of my job wheelhouse."

Nick picked up his guitar. "We can talk about it when we get back. Let's run through our duet. You got brownie cakes to make."

"Go ahead, I'm ready." Sandra smoothed out a paper on the table. "I copied the lyrics."

"Great. I'll play a short four-bar intro and you begin as the music starts to repeat." Nick strummed five chords and nodded.

Sandra hummed a moment. She sang the first stanza as Nick played the next chord.

"Great. My turn." Nick changed chords for three bars, looked at Sandra and sang.

Sandra held up three fingers, counting down the beat as Nick changed the tempo and rhythm for the chorus. Together they sang the chorus.

"Wow, both on key. Strong and great pace." Nick sat his guitar on the bench next to him. "I think we found our theme song."

Sandra laughed as she stood. "Possibly so. I'm going to get the cakes made and let Wanda know we're good with entertaining tonight."

"Sounds good. I'll straighten up in here and practice my solo. I'll be ready to go when you get back." Nick hugged Sandra to him, resting his forehead against hers briefly. "Thanks for being you. I appreciate and value what we've got."

Sandra pressed her lips to his, stepped back and winked. "You're pretty amazing too. I'm glad we've got each other and the future we're planning."

After several more hugs, kisses, and I love yous, Sandra closed the camper door behind her. Nick watched Sandra walk away until she was out of sight.

He flipped to where he left off checking chords and melody for his solo. He sang bits and pieces as he came to the changes he'd made playing the song's melody through. On the second time through, he smiled, nodding as he finished. "Yes, it's ready to go."

Nick put his guitar in its case. As he reached for the pad, his cell phone rang. Caller id showed Victor's number. Why was Victor calling?

"Hey Victor," Nick said, moving closer to the window, hoping to clear some of the staticky reception.

"There's a lot of static in the line." Victor spoke louder. "Hope's all okay. I'll be brief." Victor said two more things.

"Victor repeat. I got part of what you said. Repeat please." Nick held the phone away from his ear and a loud humming started. Victor spoke again. The noise breaking up what he said. A hum started as Victor said more—then silence. Nick lowered the phone. Nothing. No signal. No bars. The call was gone.

Nick set his phone down next to the pad. He scribbled the few words he could make out of what Victor said. Paulina and Jackson elope. Go Sylvan Valley. Gram and his mom followed? Deity on high, how had his family found them? How much did Sandra's family know?

Sandra set the two boxes of brownie mix on the prep table next to the mixing bowls Chef Ralph had put out. He put out the ingredients from the list she gave Wanda. Sandra dumped one box of brownie mix into the first bowl.

"Nice to meet you, Sandra. Please call me Ralph." Ralph placed two large sheet cake pans on the prep table. "My mom used to make a similar cake. She used melted chocolate and soft butter creamed together as a filler. If we added peppermint extract and the crushed peppermint you asked for to my mom's filler that would stretch the cakes and add a minty sweet zing to them."

"What about frosting or a topping?" Sandra cracked two eggs into the bowl. "We could sprinkle powdered sugar on top of each. What do you think?"

Ralph nodded. "Good choice. I'll get the extract and the candies."

Twenty minutes later, Sandra dried her hands on the towel Ralph handed her. They worked in tandem getting the mixes prepped and into the pans. Both sheet cake pans would take forty minutes to bake.

"Thank you, Ralph. I appreciate your help. Licking the beaters was a delicious delight. Those cakes are going to be super tasty." Sandra took the mug of tea Ralph offered her.

"I'll let you in on something. Chocolate plus peppermint is a supernatural favorite sweet treat. Most sweets are supernatural delights." Ralph saluted her with his mug. He sipped his tea and set the mug down. 'I'd like to write the recipe down for future use. Do you mind collaborating with me on the recipe?"

Sandra grinned as she set her tea mug down. "That would be awesome. Let's do it."

"Do you mind writing the recipe out? I'll type it up on the online entry form. My handwriting isn't great." Ralph handed her the pad and pen.

The first pass at the recipe was complete as the oven timer sounded. Ralph placed the two sheet pans side by side on the table.

"Wow, those smell delicious. Even better than when they were baking." Sandra saluted Ralph with her mug. "This time two cooks improved the brownie cakes."

"Collaboration. Discussing before doing. Teamwork makes the recipe work." Ralph tapped his mug to hers. "Thanks again for writing the recipe down. Let me get my computer and we'll get that entry sent off."

Sandra yawned as she opened the camper door. She hoped Nick had finished his song and was ready for a short nap cuddling. "Nick, I've got goodies." Ralph had sent back two pieces of cake from the smaller cake they'd baked with the remaining ingredients.

She set the pieces of cake on the table, looked up and gasped.

Nick's hair stood up all over his head. There was no mistaking his frown. His furled brows and scowl announced his upset better than if he'd said the words.

Sandra tossed her coat on the bench and sat down beside Nick. "What's wrong?"

Nick grabbed her, hugged her tightly to him and let go. His sigh heated the air between them. Her heart skipped one beat, then another. She rubbed her hands down her jeans twice. She started to move away as Nick reached for her hand.

"Victor called." Nick sighed. "Our peaceful interlude has party crashers en route."

"What? Please explain." Sandra pulled her hand away from Nick's.

"Paulina and Jackson are headed here. They eloped!" Nick shook his head. "Why here, I don't know. Did Victor tell them? I don't think so. Damn reception cut out before I could confirm anything."

"Are Paulina and Jackson looking for us? Can we hide out? As much as I hate to say it, avoid them?" Sandra put an arm around Nick's waist and leaned against him.

"Here's what I do know. Mom and Gram are probably following them. How soon any of them arrive is unknown." Nick reached for one of the pieces of cake. "I hope these are for us. I've got a case of the damn munchies happening."

"They're for us. Wanda said the festival potluck dinner starts at seven and entertainment at nine." Sandra put two forks and napkins on the table.

"Thanks for changing the topic." Nick picked up his fork. "I'm sorry things are cut short thanks to my family."

Sandra laid her fork down. "It's not all your family. My mother called twice while I was making the cakes. She left two voice mails wanting to know her future son-in-law's pedigree."

Nick shook his head. "I'm surprised we haven't run away from home before."

"I tried when I moved out. Moved to Witchita Falls for a couple of months. Came back for work. Living across town helps some. Sorry Nick about my mother's sizing you up like you're a stud. Breeding material." Sandra stretched. She glanced at her watch. "We've got a few hours until Ralph needs help setting up the potluck. I said I'd help."

"Ralph?" Nick finished his cake.

"Yes. The head chef. He and I collaborated on the brownie cakes. We entered our combined recipe in a cookoff in Chicago Ralph is attending next month." Sandra held up a fork full of cake. "You just enjoyed a piece."

Nick wiped his mouth. "The filling is delicious. Minty and smooth. I like the simple powder sugar topping. I wish you good luck."

Sandra ate the last bit of her piece of cake. "Thank you. Ralph is making root beer marinated ribs with cole slaw as a side dish. I think he, Chef and Pierre could upgrade Sadie's menu."

Nick smiled. "If Siobhan wants to upgrade. Her decision. I'm looking forward to meeting Ralph."

Sandra yawned. "I could use a nap. A couple more hours sleep."

"Me too. Let's get the table down and start snuggling. I know where the condoms are this time." Nick winked, adding. "If we can stay awake long enough."

Sandra blew a raspberry. "Maybe when we wake up. Energized and invigorated. Sugar flowing in all the right places?"

Nick laughed. "What about a sugar rush now?"

"Nah. Better when it's had time to ooze and flow through all the vital interested parts if you know what I mean." Sandra grinned and winked.

SIXTEEN

"You got a naughty mind." Nick ducked his head.

"Takes one to know one," Sandra bantered back.

Nick looked up, grinning. Sandra winked, coquettishly tossed her head, and blew Nick a kiss. Nick snorted, snickered and pounded the table. One peel of laughter followed by another blurted out. Their gazes met. Silence erupted, hitting heavy as it sank into being. Sandra pointed at Nick, blinked, and tried pressing her lips together firmer. Nick put his thumbs in his ears, started wiggling his fingers, crossed his eyes, and stuck out his tongue. Laughter rushed in, reclaiming its territorial hold. Sandra wrapped her arms around her stomach, laughing harder as tears rolled down her cheeks. Nick leaned on the table, laughing harder each time Sandra squeaked as she tried to stop laughing. Laughter ensued for several more moments.

"Thank you," Nick said, wiping his face. "Been a while since I laughed that hard."

"Me too." Sandra finished wiping her face. "I love we get each other's jokes."

"We're compatible in a lot of ways. Good foundation for building a long-term relationship and a match."

"Yes, it is. We didn't need a Sadie Hawkins full moon to decide." Sandra gathered their dishes and trash.

"Full moon festival tonight. Remember Wanda mentioned matchmakers are going to be there." Nick smoothed the sheets and blanket on the bunk.

"Are you hinting at a formal supernatural declaration of our relationship?" Sandra tossed the pillows on the bunk.

Nick raised her hand and pointed at the engagement ring. "We declared our intention with this twice. Good enough for me. Our families might think otherwise. Not saying either of them are overly biased."

Sandra pulled her hand away. "They sure can be narrow-visioned. Does a full moon match overrule family matchmaking?"

Nick turned, his mouth open. He closed his mouth and sat on the bunk. "Yours too?"

Sandra sat next to him, untying her hikers. "Yeah. Yours?"

Nick set his hikers next to the bunk. "Every supernatural magic chance they get. You'd think I had some special gene."

Sandra tittered. "My mother thinks you do. One of the oldest family lineages in Cauldron Falls. You'd think you were royalty."

Nick nodded. "Amongst the mixed magic shapeshifter families, we sorta are. One of my college buddies offered to do a family genetic workup. Gram said no because tinkering with magic history scientifically would let secrets out that were better off left in the past."

Sandra shucked her jeans and got under the covers. "Embellishments and family stories pair up frequently. One aunt used to say know who you are, know your health, trace back a couple of generations and let the deceased ghosts be."

"Sound advice. Except with supernaturals, there are more hybrids happening and more mashups genetically. I figure we're all mixed breeds, human or supernatural." Nick tossed his jeans next to Sandra's at the foot of the bunk. He laid the box of condoms on the counter.

Sandra yawned and turned on her side. "I'm too sleepy to decide about declaring our match. Let's talk about it when we wake up."

"Agreed." Nick spooned to Sandra, settled the covers over them, and yawned. "Sweet nap dreams."

Soft breathing sounds filtered up as sleep settled over them. One last thought bubbled up as sleep pulled Sandra deeper into its embrace. Would a full moon match declaration keep Nick's Mom and Gram from trying to break them up? They'd hinted at it when she and Nick broke up the last time.

Two Hours Later

Nick rolled over, yawned and stretched. Spooning with Sandra had an effect on him. The effect was volcanic based on certain parts of his anatomy. A hardon that demanded attention didn't like being stuffed back under the covers and whispered thoughts of maybe later. His bladder demanded attention too. Nick made his way to the bathroom, wondering if one was due to the other. Either way, he was preparing for kisses and a condom or two usage when he got back.

Sandra scooted to the edge of the bunk. She'd roused as Nick clicked the bathroom door shut. She glanced at the wall clock over the sink. Three hours until she needed to help Ralph set up. She stood as the bathroom door opened.

"Are you going to shower now or later?" Sandra turned around. Nick, a towel wrapped around his waist, approached her. "Oh, you already showered?"

"Cleaned up a bit." Nick sat on the bunk and undid part of the towel, revealing his nudity underneath. "You going to shower?"

Sandra shook her head. "Just clean up a bit. Be right back."

She grabbed her towel off the hook and closed the bathroom door. This was one of those times when wet, soap, rinse and dry quick practice runs were going to come in handy.

Nick glanced at the bathroom door as he hung up his towel. Sandra read him loud and clear. Her reaction shouted back at him as she stood. There was no mistaking her taut nipples. Definite catalytic reaction happening. He tucked two condom packets under the edge of his pillow as he lay down. He was ready to go as far as Sandra was willing to go.

Sandra reached around the open bathroom door, snagged her towel off the doorknob, and vigorously chafed her arms and legs. Cold water did nothing to douse her nipples. Only the shivers rippling up and down her arms raising goose pimples that rivaled her nipples' tightness. She tossed her towel over the door, grabbed the hand towels laying on the counter and kicked her clothes aside as she bolted toward the bed. Nick lay on his side on the outer half of the bed.

"What are you. . ." Nick reached up, placing his chilled hands close to her waist.

"Cold. Need warmth now." Sandra scrambled over Nick, tossing the towels on her pillow.

"I'll warm you up." Nick cuddled close to Sandra and covered them up. "Did you take a cold shower?"

"No, turned handle wrong way." Sandra snuggled closer to Nick. "Warming up now."

"I can warm you up even more." Nick slid his hand under the covers resting it near her breast.

"Warm your hands up first and not on me." Sandra pushed his hand away.

"I could say the same thing." Nick pulled the blanket up over their shoulders. "We need warming up inside and out. How about a few kisses in strategic places?"

He trailed his hand lower, stopping close to the top of Sandra's mons. He ruffled the hair with his fingertips. "A couple of kisses on your clit."

Sandra slid her hands lower until she reached his waist. "A couple of licks and nibbles on your cock will raise your temperature."

"Awesome minds think similar thoughts." Nick moved closer to Sandra. "Blazing hot or slow simmer to a boil?"

Sandra's hands roved lower over his hips, downward toward his erection. Patience was a virtue. One he gladly cultivated. Waiting is was his mantra. Waiting until Sandra took hold of him and suckled him between her lips. . .how long would his id cooperate? *Not too damn long dude!*

He leaned close, nipped Sandra's ear lobe and whispered. "I'm all yours."

Nick rolled onto his back. His one hand cupping her breast. Staying warm mattered. Sandra blew on her hand. "Don't think either of us is braving the cold air."

"For sure. Hard ons don't get harder in the cold. Shrink shrink shrink is not what either of us wants." Nick chuckled.

"Under the covers? My head at your groin? Your head at my mons?" Sandra started turning around.

Sandra worked her hand slowly down and around Nick until she reached the tip of his cock. "Hmm. Yes, I like." Nick groaned as her hand closed around him.

Cupping his testicles in her palm, she squeezed them softly.

Nick jerked toward her. The tip of his penis brushing against her lips.

"Ah, easy sweetie. I don't want to come yet." Nick lowered his hips.

One lick, two licks. Salty and sweet teased its way across her taste buds. Sandra held Nick with both hands, puckered her parted lips, ready to french kiss his cock. Up and down, her tongue laving in short strokes as she bobbed her head. Tightening her lips on her upward suckle, she recupped Nick's testicles, palming them as she sucked him into her mouth again.

Nick grasped part of the sheet, bunching it into his hands. Fire erupted deep inside him every stroke and suckle Sandra completed. On her last stroke upward, his balls constricted against him. His cock swelled and...One blast of semen followed by another shot out of him. Reds, blues and golds erupted behind his closed eyes in firework arrays. Each brighter than the first until the colors faded and his mind cleared.

Sandra wiped her hands with a towel. She curled up tight to Nick, laying her head on his shoulder. "Nice to know I haven't lost my touch."

"You sure haven't. Whoa, that was damn fine." Nick let go a deep sigh. "You ready for stars and fireworks?"

Sandra blew him a kiss and winked. "Sure you up to it?"

Nick licked his fingertip, trailed it around Sandra's nipple twice, and down over her stomach, stopping short of the apex of her legs. He arched an eyebrow, tilted his head and nodded. "Oh, I am up to it. Are you up to it?"

Sandra exhaled slowly. She was wet already. Anticipation—Nick touching her very close to her clit, and—her nipples couldn't get any stiffer, could they? If Nick remembered how to set off her multiple orgasms the last time both of them were this turned on, her fireworks fuse would burn hotly with compound waves.

She covered Nick's hand with hers. "Up to it, yes. Able to do more afterward, probably not. Blissed out and dozing, more than likely."

"Let's see what happens." Nick nipped her earlobe, suckling it between his lips. He let go and whispered. "Your clitoris is next."

Sandra shivered, gulped and closed her eyes. Waves of desire surged through her, pulsating over her nipples, deep into her middle igniting smaller pulses echoing upward and down until Nick fondled her nipples as he kissed her clit—Volcanic orgasms producing internal and external body quakes of varying magnitudes were possible.

Nick nipped his way down her neck, stopping at her shoulder. He worried the area close to the base of her throat between his teeth. He let go, kissing the area and blowing across it. Tiny shivers rumpled down and over her.

"Delicious. More deliciousness here." Nick dragged his wet fingertip down and over her nipple, catching it with his thumb and forefinger. Thug. Twist. Repeating several more times until. . .Nick let go and straddled her.

Nick leaned forward, placing his hands on either side of her waist. Steadying himself on his hands, he slowly slid one leg down hers until his knee rested between hers. He lowered his head, captured her nipple closest to him and suckled. He worried the nipple with his teeth and let go. Sandra sucked her stomach in. Blasts of need whirled tighter and upon each other ready to set off a tornadic wave of ecstasy. How much longer could she hold out? Her clit was as taut as her nipples.

Nick slid his other leg over and down her leg until he rested on his elbows and knees. He let go of her nipple, blew on his wet handiwork and lowered himself until his chest and her mons rubbed against each other. "Heat. Wetness. Chemistry for sure. Let's see what else is waiting to detonate."

Nick looped his arms around her legs as he settled between her legs, his face close to her vulva. He looked up, parted his lips and ducked his head. One hasty tickle of his tongue over the tip of her clit.

Sandra clenched bunches of the sheet and covers in her hands. If he kept this up, she would orgasm from sheer desire. Did she look? Push up against him, saying what she wanted? She started to open her hands and relax.

SEVENTEEN

"Nick! Oh yes!" Two fast licks followed by one slow lazy lave over and around. The combination continued as Nick inserted his finger into her until he found her g-spot. He suckled her between his lips, flicking his tongue rapidly over her while massaging her g-spot. White light mixed with reds, oranges, and purples exploded in tight spirals. Each overlapping the other, mixing with no beginning or ending. The colors began to fade.

Sandra slowly inhaled, opened her eyes and looked down. Nick held up two fingers, nodding and ducked his head again. An unhurried tongue lave lingered across her clit, pausing every time she jerked. Nick kept up his focused intent as one more orgasmic blast shuddered through her. She slumped on the mattress, orgasmically blissed out. She was done. Ready to sleep and soon. "No more," she managed to blurt out. "Sleep please."

Nick wiped his hands and face on the other towel, tossed them both on the floor and pulled the covers over them as he lay beside Sandra. One thought filled him. No one responded to him like Sandra. No other woman filled his heart and mind. She was the one. Gram and Mom were going to have a fight on their hands if they thought otherwise.

An Hour Later

Nick brushed his lips over Sandra's. "Hate to break up the cuddle. We gotta get ready for the festival."

Sandra nodded and stretched. "You showering first or am I?"

Nick pulled the covers higher. "Wish there was enough room in there for us to shower together. Save time and water."

"Yeah, right. We'd be so late and run out of hot water. I had enough cold earlier." Sandra dragged her fingers down his chest.

"You want me to go first." Nick popped the covers up and down.

"No fair. That's cold." Sandra grabbed at the blanket.

"Prepping for when I gotta skitter to the bathroom and turn the heater up." Nick rolled to the edge of the bunk and sat up.

"You turned the heater down?" Sandra wrapped the blanket around her as she sat up.

"No. Keep the temperature level as nightfalls." Nick stood. "I need fifteen minutes to shower and dress. You?"

"About the same. You dressing up for this?" Sandra worked her hair into a loose bun.

"Jeans, long-sleeved t-shirt and sweatshirt. Nothing fancy."

Sandra scooted to the edge of the bunk. "Wanda mentioned due to weather, everything changed to the community center."

"Good. Easier to sing when your teeth aren't chattering."

Sandra waited until she heard the bathroom door click shut before she stood up. Trying to keep the blanket wrapped around her wasn't easy. She clutched at parts of it as she stooped to pick up her and Nick's clothes plus the hand towels. They were going to need to do laundry if they were going to stay the full week. Would it be possible with Nick's family en route plus her mother threatening to publicize her daughter's wedding in the society pages of the larger newspapers in the adjoining states?

Choices. . . what did one wear when they were on stage? The few concerts she attended performers wore jeans and t-shirts. Work events she dressed in slacks, blouse and blazer or a dress or skirt. This wasn't a work event. Casual was what she had. Casual it was.

She laid her clothes on the bunk next to where Nick had tossed his. Her sweatshirt with the full moon night sky on it would fit right in. A long sleeve top and jeans. Nothing fancy. Nothing to call attention to them.

She straightened up the bunk as Nick opened the bathroom door. Her hand closed around the condom packets. Two days out from her cycle and no cramps. PMS visited her with regularity every month. No moodiness. No cravings. Could she have caught that fast? Only effective birth control per her doctor was holding an aspirin between her knees all night and yelling no. Sandra closed her eyes, murmured a quick prayer, and unclenched her hand. Neither of them would know for sure until she took a pregnancy test once they returned to Cauldron Falls.

"Next," Nick said by-passing her. "Plenty of warm water."

"Thanks," Sandra muttered, moving by Nick quickly.

Nick hung his towel up. Something was bothering Sandra. She hadn't made eye contact or had a comeback about warm water instead of hot. She liked her showers steamy and extra warm. Asking her what was up would have to wait. Duty, as his Mom called it, came first.

"Yeah, right." Nick pulled his jeans and t-shirt on. He needed to get over to the community center, check out the sound system and help set up the tables and chairs. Sandra would be helping Ralph. Not much time for private chatter until they got back. Nick tied his hikers, put on his sweatshirt and stood. He turned, a patch of silver caught his eye. The condom packets lay near the pillows. Oh, crap. Pregnancy scare had tripped Sandra. Why couldn't Paulina and Jackson elope to Las Vegas or someplace else? Why Sylvan Valley?

"Sandra, are you okay?" Nick started toward the bathroom as the door opened.

"Some what." Sandra held her hands out in front of her. "Too much happening all at once again. Feels like the paparazzi are lurking everywhere. I know they're not."

"Family and paparazzi are like piranha at times. Waiting to latch on and sink their teeth into you." Nick spread his arms wide. "Need a hug?"

"Maybe after I dress." Sandra scooted by him. "My mind is what if this, what if that. It's the damn unknowns that are messing with me."

"How about a quick snack before we head out for the festival?" Nick held up a package of peanut butter crackers. He put two mugs of water in the microwave as he continued talking. "Plus a quick cup of chamomile tea. I snitched two tea bags when I was talking to Wanda earlier."

"Exactly what I need." Sandra quickly dressed. She sat on the bunk, brushing her hair. "I need to ask a question."

Nick squatted down in front of her. "Ask away."

"What if your family doesn't approve of me?" Sandra leaned back on her hands.

"I wonder the same about yours." Nick sat beside her. "The real question is who are we marrying? Committing to? Each other or our families?"

Sandra snickered. "Our families are part of us no matter what. Marrying—That's you and I if we go through with it."

Nick stood as the microwave buzzed. "I made my commitment to you when I proposed both times. We've talked about kids in the past. I want them, want them with you, and that isn't changing."

Sandra stood, took Nick's hand and tugged him to her. She looped her arms around his neck, snuggling as close as their stance permitted. "Thank you. I made my commitment twice too. Our kids are going to have a lot of love and caring happening with us as parents."

"They sure are." Nick hugged her and let go. "Now let's snack."

The next fifteen minutes passed quietly except for the rustling of the cellophane wrapper and spoons stirring honey into the tea. Calm pervaded the air, sending skepticism packing. Sandra sighed as she set her empty mug in the sink. Maybe this was what believing in love was all about. Trusting each other plus themselves to speak their truths, not stifle or hide their emotions. Taking the leap of faith and seeing it multipled because together they were stronger and united than either of them individually was.

Nick cupped her face, massaging her head with his fingertips. "I know you can hold your own. I trust you. There's magics and mortals here that don't care if we're mortal, magic or hybrid. Sylvan Valley's citizens treat each other with dignity and respect. Everyone has something to contribute."

"Sound like a great place to live and bring up your kids." Sandra turned her head, pressing her lips against Nick's hand. "Together or a part, we're strong. Our trust is mutual. I love you."

"I love you, too." Nick lowered his hands, leaned closer and brushed his lips over hers. "Now we got festival work to do."

Hand in hand, they walked toward the main building. Nick squeezed her hand and let go as they reached the door. Sandra rubbed her hands on the inside of her pockets. Bits of perspiration dotted parts of the material. Her calm and worry nipped at each other, working to dominate each other. Who would top the other? She bet both would be looking for a place to hide when Nick's Mom and Gram arrived. Their staunch and rather staid reputations left little to the imagination. Sandra snorted as one last thought crossed her mind as she entered the lobby. Her mother wanted a long lineage, pedigreed son-in-law. What a mash-up her mother plus Nick's mom and gram would be.

Sandra entered the lobby. She faced Nick. "Are you ready for your mom and gram?"

Nick grasped Sandra's hand and kissed her cheek; close to her ear, he whispered. "Are *we* ready for Mom and Gram?"

"We?"

"Yes. We. Us. You and me." He pulled back, winked and let go of Sandra's hand. "I believe we're ready. Do you?"

"I think we are. We trust ourselves, our hearts and our bond is strong." Sandra cupped his cheek. "Family is special. Our strongest bond. Our ingrained home. Stepping away from that takes courage."

Nick turned and pressed a kiss into Sandra's palm. He moved back as he spoke. "Moving on is a major part of our lives. We've done quite a bit of it ourselves. Now it's time for you and I do it together."

Sandra nodded. "Time to build our life together. Believe in love and trust the bond it's created for us."

"For sure, sweetheart." Nick glanced at his watch. "I'm helping Hal set up the sound system for tonight. Text me if you need anything."

Nick walked away, picking up pace as Hal came around the registration desk. Sandra watched the two of them chattering as they exited the lobby. She'd learned two important things over the last few days. Nick lit up when he talked about playing music and sang. His enthusiasm pulsed outward as he described setting up for impromptu concerts or rehearsals when he opened for other well-known country rock artists. Music got Nick juicy. It was his calling.

"Ready to decorate and set up the banquet tables?"

Sandra startled, turning around quickly. "Ralph, sneaking up on me?"

"Sorry. Thought you saw and heard me." Ralph pushed the cart laden with boxes and vases forward. High-pitched squeaks sounded.

"Caught up in my thoughts." Sandra pointed at the cart. "Is there more?"

"Last load. Hal and I took most of it over before lunch. Wanda's sister Caroline and her husband Anders took over the heavier load in their truck." Ralph glanced over his shoulder. "Wanda wanted to know what you and I planned for the prize money if our recipe won the bake-off contest."

Sandra grinned. "Split it. Bank it. Spend it. Fold it in half to double it real quick."

Ralph chortled, pushing the cart toward the hall marked Rest Rooms and Exit. "Good one. I like the fold it in half. Does double funds quickly."

"How far is the community center from here?" Sandra pushed the exit door open.

"A short walk outside the side exit. Main entrance is off Cedar Street. You probably passed it coming in." Ralph shoved the cart over the door frame. The top two boxes pitched back and forth.

"I've got 'em." Sandra steadied both boxes and picked them up.

"Thanks. Decorations. Not many looking at them. Busy sizing up the competition or the food more." Ralph turned left, continuing down the walkway.

"Makes good business for the matchmaker." Sandra moved up alongside Ralph.

"Yeah, my wife Tracey thinks so. She's the matchmaker. I get most of the referrals from her." Ralph pulled a set of keys from his pocket.

"Seems fair. You get to cater the receptions and pair bondings."

"When you're what the mortal refer to as the justice of the peace, you're busy with officiating more than planning receptions." Ralph unlocked the community center's front doors.

EIGHTEEN

"Justice of the Peace?" Sandra followed him into the community center's lobby.

"Yup, got plenty of marriage licenses in one box. Good thing the state has no waiting period." Ralph pointed to the door to their left. "Kitchen is through there. Dining and meeting area is through the double doors next to it."

Sandra followed Ralph across the lobby toward the open door leading to the kitchen.

"Test. Test", sounded, followed by an off-key voice singing, "Your heart is sweeter than wine."

Sandra looked at Ralph, shook her head and grinned. "Hope the singer isn't going for first prize."

"Hal knows better. He's a great accountant. Whiz at mayoring Sylvan Falls. Awesome singer, he ain't." Ralph pushed the cart into the kitchen. "Hal figures the day he sounds on key; the sound system is shot."

Sandra snickered. "One way to ensure you know if things are working."

Ralph chortled and nodded. "Yes and another reason why we don't ask him to sing the national anthem at the opening of sports season."

Sandra tittered as Hal singing again flooded out of the sound system. Nick's voice followed. "Hal, I think we can turn the volume down more."

Ralph unloaded most of the cart onto the prep table. "The boxes you have go on the table labeled matchmaker and JP. Why don't you help Tracey and Caroline with the decorating? Anders and I will finish setting up the tables."

Sandra carried the two boxes into the dining area. "Hi, I'm Sandra. I'm looking for Tracey and Caroline."

A tall blonde and a brunette stood behind a table near the front of the room turned.

The blonde waved. "I'm Caroline. Nice to meet you. This is Tracey."

The brunette smiled and moved around the table she stood behind. "Can I help you with the boxes?"

"Ralph said they needed to go on the matchmaker and JP's table." Sandra let go of the box Tracey took hold of.

"Ralph loves to be prepared. His JP cloak is in one box. You never know if marriage licenses will be needed or not. Most folks choose a full moon ceremony and get on with things." Tracey set the box on a small table close to the larger long table she and Caroline had been standing behind.

"We're expecting a full house tonight. Half the town has rsvp'd for the potluck. Many will show up for the dessert run before the talent show." Caroline held up the seating diagram. "Food tables are close to the kitchen. Main seating begins along the back wall with six long tables to a row and fifteen seats to a side. Easier to turn chairs around when the show starts."

Sandra pointed to the two empty spots on the diagram. "What is going there?"

"Cashier's station, full moon match ticket sales, and donation jar for the lodge renovation fund. Expand the community center, upgrade city council wing, and down payments on wi-fi towers." Caroline pointed to another open section closer to the front of the auditorium. "Private JP ceremonies or full moon match bondings area."

Tracey picked up the box of decorations. "Anders and Ralph are setting up tables from the back to the front. Table runners and a small vase for each table. We can place the flowers once the table is decorated."

Forty-five minutes passed as Sandra worked in tandem with Tracey taping the table runners down and placing a small vase middle of each table. Caroline directed Anders and Ralph where the tables went.

Anders opened the water bottle Caroline handed him and drank half of it. "Ralph, if the whole town shows up, this place is going to be packed."

Ralph sat on the folding chair close to the JP and Matchmaker table, sipping his water. "Nothing wrong with that. Tracey and I are doing ceremonies out around the bond fire pit. When Sylvan Valley comes together, love magic happens. Love the energy, friendship and support the community pulses when we all come together."

Tracey patted Ralph's shoulder. "I suggest we put a waiting list together for the JP ceremonies. I'm going to need your help if a large number turn out for full moon bondings."

"You got it, dear. Renewals or first-time bondings got priority. Might do that mix of JP and matchmaker ceremony we used last month in Cameron Valley."

Caroline hugged Anders. "That got rave reviews. I think you might want to go with that tonight. Lots of folks are mixed couples, mortal and magic. Even supernatural and mortal or magic."

Ralph rose. "Sounds like a winner. Tracey, you on board with that?"

"Sure, full moon bonding comes first. Invoking Luna and the One requires the special prayer and bonding spell." Tracey picked up one of the floral bouquets out of the vase on the main front table. "Each table gets two flowers. No two are alike. See what moves you as you set them out."

Sandra took part of the bouquet. "Sometimes it all comes down to believing. Believing your heart, believing in yourself and the magic of love."

"So be it," Ralph declared, taking part of another bouquet from Tracey. "First one done gets to help me with registering civil ceremonies."

Fifteen minutes passed as Sandra, Tracey and Caroline placed the first flower in each vase on the thirty tables. Anders and Ralph followed with the second flowers.

"We're done here." Caroline glanced at her watch. "Thirty minutes until people start arriving. I'm gonna shower and change. Anders and I will see you at six-thirty."

Ralph nodded. "Tracey and I need to change into our officiant clothes. We'll be back about the same time."

"I'm going to see if Nick and Hal need help." Sandra followed Tracey, Ralph, Caroline and Anders into the lobby. "See you at six-thirty."

Nick looked up from the soundboard and mixing station. "Hal, you've got a home recording studio here. How come you haven't launched any recordings?"

"Time and energy plus money. Wanda and I bought the lodge and campgrounds from her grandfather. He dabbled in radio broadcasting, recording local folks, and promoting their stuff locally. Winfred Goddard and Mitchell Nieves hit the state big stations. They went on to short-lived careers."

"I met Mitchell a few years ago at the state fair in Witchita Falls. Nice fellow. He had a trio that put on a couple of shows. I sang back up and played guitar for one of the shows. Found my calling, music and singing." Nick put the soundboard on standby.

"Glad you're performing tonight. How many songs?" Hal picked up the clipboard holding the talent show roster.

"Two. Sandra and I are doing a duet. The second song is one I recently wrote." Nick pointed at the clipboard. "What's the schedule look like?"

"If you and Sandra don't mind headlining, I'd appreciate you opening the show. I can put you on toward the end with the choral group's piano player and backup band." Hal showed Nick the lineup.

"A few locals singing and storytelling. Some comedy and the local choral group. A real variety show." Nick pointed to an open spot toward the end of the list. "I'll take that spot for my solo. Gives me time to write down the chords and percussion for the piano and backup band."

"Great! You'll close out the show." Hal wrote Nick's name in the open space. "Food service starts at seven-thirty. Show starts at nine. See you in thirty minutes."

"Okay Hal. See you in a half hour. Time to get my guitar and lyrics. See what Sandra is up to." Nick exited the sound booth.

Sandra was waiting for him as he entered the auditorium. "All done setting up?"

"Yeah. I met Ralph's wife and her sister and husband." Sandra held up her phone. "I got a strange text from Victor and a text from *my mother*."

Nick read Victor's text aloud. "M and G right behind P and J. Sorry, no time to forewarn." Nick flexed his hands and continued speaking. "Frack. What did your mom say?"

Sandra sighed. "Mother somehow tracked us down. She's en route. To which I say double frack!"

Nick hugged Sandra to him. "How do we prepare for this family showdown?"

"I say we don't. Evade and improvise." Sandra returned his hug. "Let's enjoy the harmony and tranquility while we still got it."

"Agree. I've got to prep music for the piano and backup band Hal is matching me up with for my solo." Nick held Sandra's hand.

"I knew there was a reason I kept the chamomile tea back. A cup might help calm the agitation ready to burst forth." Sandra let go of his hand and moved toward the exit.

Nick followed, pressing his fingers against his legs repeatedly. Some said full moons brought out the loons. Birds he didn't mind. Manipulative family members he and Sandra didn't need.

Thursday Night

Nick propped his guitar against the chair next to him. Ninety minutes of peace and not a word about what they were going to do when their moms and gram plus Paulina and Jackson arrived.

The potluck food was fabulous. Sandra and Ralph's brownie cakes had several attendees asking for the recipe. Topping a slice of cake with homemade ice cream put him into a tranquil state of mind. His stomach gurgled its contentment after his second helpings.

Sandra was busy clearing tables and helping Tracey with names for full moon bondings. Nick had asked Sandra about taking the leap here and now with full moon bonding and a JP ceremony. Bind their troth supernaturally and mortally. Sandra had stared at him, her mouth moving, nothing coming out. He'd kissed her cheek and whispered, "Later."

Seated next to the stage, ready for the entertainment to begin, Nick scanned the crowd. No sign of Paulina and Jackson or Gram and Mom. Sandra hadn't seen her mother amongst the guests gathering for the talent show.

"How soon do we go on?" Sandra handed him his guitar and sat on the chair next to him.

"Hal said about ten minutes." Nick slipped his arm through the guitar's strap. "Get a lot of names for either ceremony?"

"Ralph has a few for tonight. More interested in vow and relationship renewals referrals than anything else." Sandra tossed her empty water bottle in the trash bin close to the stage. "Tracey has several full moon bonding ceremonies for tonight. She and Ralph are using a combined full moon and legal bonding ceremony to fit everyone in. Everyone is a witness for everyone else."

"Awesome idea. Have you given more thought to us joining that group?" Nick emptied his water bottle and tossed it in the trash can.

"Part of me is on board. Part of me doesn't like feeling like our families are pushing us." Sandra held up her hand as Nick opened his mouth. "Believing in us, in our bond and commitment and our love outweighs the feeling pushed part."

"Nothing says we have to do anything other than what we feel is right." Nick stood as Hal came out on stage. "I pray Paulina and Jackson use Mom and

Gram as their witnesses elsewhere. And that your mother safely gets to your cousin's leaving us a day or two more peace instead of bits and pieces of chaos."

"Agreed. Loving your family doesn't mean you have to accept everything they do." Sandra released his hand.

"Sylvan Valley citizens are we ready for entertainment?" Hal held the microphone out, picking up the cheers and shouts of the audience. "All right, our opening act is a duet by our visitors from Cauldron Falls, Nick and Sandra!"

NINETEEN

Applause broke out as Nick started up the stage steps. He noted Sandra was right behind him. He waited until she was beside him before continuing to where two microphones were stage center. He plugged in the cord from the amplifier to his guitar, strummed a few notes, and faced the crowd.

"Evening everyone. We'd like to share with you a duet I wrote called Together Again." Nick strummed the opening notes and chords, looked at Sandra and nodded.

Sandra wet her lips and sang:
"Look at us standing here together.
Who knew what happened?
It was magical.
You and me belong together.
I knew I'd never go anywhere without you.
Time always stops when I look at you."
Nick played the opening notes of the second stanza and sang:
"You and me side by side.
Our connection is stronger this time.
Who knew how magical it could be?
What our hearts and our minds denied?
Will it work out this time?
Or are we fooling ourselves?"
His and Sandra's gazes met as Nick played the bridge and intro to the chorus. Together they sang, smiling and not looking away:
"Together again,
Do we want to take the step?
Our hearts keep saying yes.
Do we listen to our minds say no?
Are we stronger enough to make it last?
Accepting what our hearts say with every beat,
Together is our fate."
Nick strummed the final chords and notes. Loud applause sounded. He and Sandra clasped hands and bowed.

Hal introduced the next act, a choral group from the local high school. They sang a medley of show tunes followed by two favorite local songs. The next four acts offered comedy, storytelling and more singing. Fifty minutes of quality local entertainment.

Hal held up a sheet of paper as the last group of entertainers left the stage. "Folks, Tracey and Ralph have a few openings left for the combination JP and Full Moon bonding ceremony they're conducting at the full moon pinnacle at eleven."

Wolf whistles and cheers followed and quieted down as Hal held up his hands. "All right enough. You can schedule your own. Talk with Ralph and Tracey."

The audience quieted down as the spotlight shined down on Hal. "Closing out our show tonight with his newest solo song is Nick."

The spotlight shifted from Hal to Nick. Nick bowed and waved as the applause died down. "Thank you everyone. Tonight's talent was awesome. Great comedy sketches. Loved the animated storytelling. The choral group was fantabulous!"

More applause and whistles signaled the attendees' agreement. Nick pulled up a stool Hal placed next to him and perched on it. "Writing music and singing are joyous things for me. A Sadie Hawkins full moon love magic is wonderous. Adding Luna and the One's matchmaking bond to it can catch you off-guard. Sometimes you don't hear what your heart is saying. Believe in Love is dedicated to my Sadie Hawkins full moon match and bond."

Behind Nick, the opening piano chords sounded, followed by a rhythmic drum beat and the electronic sounds of the base guitar mixed in. Nick played the lead melody and sang.

"Love can be elusive.

Strange things we don't notice,

Until we listen to our hearts.

Girl, you walked into my heart,

Settled down and knew what you wanted,

Too bad I didn't.

Can you forgive me?

I'm learning to listen to my heart.

Listen to my heart.

Know it's right.
Listen to the words it says.
With each beat telling me
One thing, you're the one.
I'd apologize, but you'd say no need.
'Cuz you needed to listen to your heart.
We both needed to see,
What our hearts knew from the start.
We're the one each of us sought.
Believe in love, my heart and yours kept saying.
Listen and know what you been missing.
Have faith and stop denying.
Believe in love and what your heart is saying.
It's time to start listening to our hearts.
Hear the words they say with each beat.
Listen to the words our psyches repeat.
Love is what is meant to be.
Listening to our hearts will get us there.
"There's only one answer.
My heart knows what I haven't said,
I'm in love.
How could I miss what was right before me?
It's you, only you.
Others came and went.
You moved and stayed.
No other ignites my heart like you.
Now I believe in love,
I hope you do too,
'Cuz what our hearts showed us is true.
Believing in love all we need to do."

Applause erupted as Nick sang the last note. The spotlight swept out over the crowd, pausing on Sandra and sweeping back toward the stage. . .*Paulina and Jackson? They were here already?* Victor's last text said they weren't due for another two days. Crap. Double crap. Did that mean Mom and Gram . . .

The spotlight arced out over the whole audience in one final sweep. Nick shoved his hands into his jeans back pockets. Come on Luna and the One, why here? Why now? Mom and Gram were two rows back from Paulina and Jackson!

The audience was on their feet yelling encore. Hal walked up to the mike as full stage lights came on. "If we had the time, Nick might sing another song. It's after ten. Tracey and Ralph could use help setting up the bonding circle. Anders and I are looking for a couple of volunteers to help us get the bond fire going. Luna is ready to shine down and bless matches and civil unions."

Wanda joined Hal on the stage. "Everyone participating in the bonding and civil union ceremony, you've got about twenty-five minutes to change and join the circle. The rest, if you are attending the ceremony, please take your chair outside with you."

Nick stepped back until he was at the perimeter of the stage close to the steps. Paulina and Jackson were making their way over to Ralph. People milling around blocked Gram and Mom's view of them. Nick exhaled slowly. A showdown was probably inescapable. Many clan and family members referred to Gram and Mom as bullheaded, unwilling to change or flex. Luna, strong leadership helped the magics and supernaturals survive in the past. The new order leadership understood the need for change. Nick hoped his mom and gram would eventually make peace with the change and move forward with welcoming Sandra and his children with open arms, not wanting to test for latent magic genetics.

Nick scanned the crowd, locating Sandra making her way to where Tracey and Ralph were talking with Paulina and Jackson. As Nick moved closer to the stage steps, he halted. Gram and Mom were rushing at him, pointing at him, saying something. The inevitable showdown had begun.

"Sandra!" Her mother was here? Sandra glanced behind her, pressed her lips together and took off running. Her mother called her name again. Sandra picked up pace by passing two women fighting their way through the crowd toward the stage.

Sandra dodged left, bumping into Caroline. "Sorry. Gotta get to Nick. Pains closing in fast."

Caroline nodded and called out. "Anders evasive maneuvers now."

Anders grabbed Sandra's hand. "Come on. I'll lift you up on the stage as close to Nick as I can get you."

Sandra faced Anders. "I'm with you. Let's do it."

Anders grasped her around the waist, walked her backward until her back pressed against the edge of the elevated stage. His gaze met hers. "Ready. On three up you go."

"One—Two—Three!" Anders hefted her up high enough for her to sit on the stage and scoot back.

"Thanks." Sandra scooted back more, calling out as she did. "Nick, I'm ready. Let's do it!"

Nick clutched both of her hands, helping her to her feet. "Are you sure? This is for real. Nothing fake happening."

"It's time for us. Our decision matters. I'm sure. The combined ceremony bonds us legally and magically. Our families can contest all they want. Are you sure?"

"As sure as this," Nick let go of one hand and tugged her toward the exit at the back of the stage leading to the loading dock. "Sandra, let's go get full moon bonded and legally hitched."

Caroline met them at the loading dock steps. "Your full moon bonding candles, cloaks and Ralph prefilled your marriage certificate. Luna and the One bless you. Blessed Be!"

"Thanks Caroline! Appreciate you and Anders's help." Nick held one cloak out to Sandra. "Time to light our bonding candles and join the ceremony circle."

Sandra slipped the cloak on. "What do the cloaks and candles symbolize?"

"Women and men are partners of the clan." Nick put his cloak on, belting it around his waist. "Luna and the One unite the supernatural and magic into a unique force called love. The heart weaves a special force around those it embraces and the families they create."

"It's like the saying it takes a village to raise a family. We all bring a particular talent to the mix." Sandra took the white and silver candle from Nick. "Silver for the starlight? White for moonlight?"

Nick took Sandra's hand. "Yes. We'll light the candles from the bond fire and join the ceremony circle."

Hand in hand they made their way to the bond fire, lighting their candles and faced the center of the circle as they joined it. Nick glanced around the circle, noting the illuminated faces. Paulina and Jackson were opposite them on the other side of the circle, close to where the observers and extra witnesses stood. Nick squinted, focusing his gaze on two people close to the edge of the group behind Paulina and Jackson. Luna, please let Mom and Gram hold their tongues. He scanned the crowd more. A woman caught his attention. She stood directly behind the second row of seats. She looked familiar. He nudged Sandra. "Is that your mother?"

Sandra shielded her eyes, glancing from right to left and back. She dropped her hand, letting go an exasperated sigh. "Yes. Your mom and gram are in the crowd too."

Nick grasped her hand, kissed each knuckle and let go. "They can't accuse us of faking anything."

Sandra snickered. "My mother probably won't. She'll be fawning and preening as she awaits her introduction. Your mom and gram—there's no telling."

As much as he wished what Sandra said wasn't true, he knew better. Would Mom and Gram clam up and walk away? He doubted it. Ignore him and Sandra? Probably not. Maybe they might forego the inquisition some family members accused them of. Pounce on Paulina and Jackson? No telling. Divide and pounce? Good possibility. Mom come after him and Sandra. Gram after Paulina and Jackson.

Nick leaned close to Sandra and whispered. "I know two things for sure."

"What's that?"

"I love you. I'm glad we're getting married." Nick squeezed Sandra's hand.

Sandra smiled and nodded. "Me too."

Tracey held her candle up. "All those in the circle, please raise your candles."

As the candles rose and the clouds parted, a candlelight halo and moonbeams illuminated the circle and its occupants.

Tracey moved to one side of the bond fire spoke. "Luna, many join tonight, forming a commitment to each other. A partnership founded on love and caring. May those who pledge and bond tonight honor each other through good and bad. Through health and illness. Coming together as partners and family if children happen with the understanding, respect and dignity are basic to all things. In the name of the One, bless those renewing their vows and confirm their continued bond for as long as it lasts. So be it. Luna and the One be praised."

Murmurs of 'So be it' echoed from the group as Ralph joined Tracey. He held up his candle. "Legal ceremony requires papers and vows said before a justice of the peace. I am the justice of the peace representing the state and Sylvan Valley. All who have a legal paper they are signing as proof of their marriage are hear by pronounced pair bonded and wed."

"None of these bondings are recognized by the clans. A third-generation matchmaker witch is not officiating," a voice called out. Nick cringed. His mom stepped into the center of the circle.

"They are sanctified by the matchmakers' council and my coven." Tracey reached into her cloak and held out the pendant she wore. "I am a member of the third-degree coven, blessed and consecrated by the matchmakers' council as well. I am the third daughter of a third witch of a third-generation mage."

"I will perform any legal ceremony needed for those that want them." Ralph held Tracey's hand.

Nick stepped into the circle. Sandra right with him. He faced his mom and gram. "Sandra and I are bonded. Married. That isn't going to change. You can welcome us into the family or lose us. The choice is yours."

EPILOGUE

Ten Months Later

Nick laid his guitar on the couch. Tickets were selling out for the second leg of his cross-country tour. His single, Believe in Love, hit the top one hundred on country and rock charts. Radio stations were vying for interviews and publicity offers. Lenny kept saying he was on his way to the big time. Success and more fame. It paled next to what he and Sandra had.

Mom and Gram were coming around despite not talking to them for four months. They'd swooped down on Paulina and Jackson the moment Paulina announced her pregnancy. They didn't believe Sandra when she announced her pregnancy until she took two pregnancy tests and both came out positive. His mom and gram had sent gifts for Sandra's baby shower and notes discussing possible future visits.

Sandra's family reunion had gone better than either of them had anticipated. Her mother stopped asking about genealogy and magic history after several of Sandra's family recognized him and knew members of his family. One cousin told Sandra's mother marrying into one of Cauldron Falls' oldest magic families was a feat that didn't need advertising. Nick didn't blame his mother-in-law for wanting to know about him. Gram and Mom kept wanting to know more about Sandra. Each would learn more as they interacted with their new grandkids and great-grandkids.

Jackson had covertly asked Victor if his camper was available for another escape. Victor's no surprised everyone. A few cousins said Victor's great Aunt Agatha had her eye on getting him matched. Where Victor had disappeared to no one knew. Nick hoped he was enjoying the camper and what solitude he could get. Aunt Agatha and Aunt Stella weren't going to let up. Even his cousin Ryan was on the two aunts' matchmaking list.

Sandra's pregnancy hadn't been easy. Morning sickness in reverse for the last trimester had both of them wondering what else could happen. Ultrasounds didn't show the twins until five months into the pregnancy. Unsure of either baby's sex, they'd come up with different names and possible blends of first and middle names. Through it all, their love had grown deeper and stronger.

Sandra laid Emily in her bassinet next to her twin brother Samuel. Nick rose, slipped his arm around Sandra's waist and hugged her tightly as he whispered, "I won't stop believing in love. It's a wonderful blessing."

Sandra turned to him. She cupped his cheek. "Neither will I stop believing in the love we've found and got."

THE END

Don't miss out!

Visit the website below and you can sign up to receive emails whenever Solara Gordon publishes a new book. There's no charge and no obligation.

https://books2read.com/r/B-A-RAUJ-CPHHC

BOOKS 2 READ

Connecting independent readers to independent writers.

Did you love *Believe In Love*? Then you should read *Falling for You*[1] by Solara Gordon!

[2]

Mutual chemistry, connection and a mischievous dachshund named McGee equals a great first date, right? Not for neighbors Drake and Sara. When a cold snap and snowstorm forces Drake and Sara together under one roof, their attraction ignites sparks of desire. Is their prospective date turning into a unique first date or more?

Read more at https://solaragordon.com/.

1. https://books2read.com/u/bOJeOg

2. https://books2read.com/u/bOJeOg

Also by Solara Gordon

Watch for more at https://solaragordon.com/.

www.ingramcontent.com/pod-product-compliance
Lightning Source LLC
Chambersburg PA
CBHW060650260626
47161CB00008B/3073